Where Angels Tread

Michael Reisman

iUniverse, Inc.
New York   Bloomington

Where Angels Tread

iUniverse books may be ordered through booksellers or by contacting:

iUniverse
1663 Liberty Drive
Bloomington, IN 47403
www.iuniverse.com
1-800-Authors (1-800-288-4677)

ISBN: 978-1-4401-2532-4 (pbk)
ISBN: 978-1-4401-2533-1 (ebk)

Printed in the United States of America

iUniverse rev. date: 02/16/2009

one young special lady...

one young special lady sat before me at the age of fifteen. she was an aspiring writer who just read a few stories from my first published book. her eyes glowed with the intensity of a mature woman and she put her arms around my neck with a hug that said thank you. I got mail from her saying that her English teacher now reads one story a day to her class at school. my heart swelled with pride knowing that I have touched someone in a very special way. and so does wisdom often speak from the mouth of children who learn and teach us well. my second book will be dedicated to this sweet young soul who has taught me about a simple hug and loving eyes that can be spread to others. for you Sara, I may be now the student and you the teacher. let me be the first in line where I may have your autograph...

just one stop after...

the train ride to work was about 45 minutes as two passengers took their same seat out of habit. she would chat on her cell phone and he would read a book, both passing the time. just before they got off at the same stop, each would look at the other and smile a goodbye until the following morning. she turned off her cell phone and he put the unopened book down on the seat next to him. maybe it was time for a day not to go to work as both of them needed something more than a weekly paycheck.

it was one stop after that the two of them got off the train and walked in no particular direction. for some reason they held hands as if they already knew each other. it turned out that both had the same summer vacation schedule and met on that same week. despite the difference in age and the way they dressed or the language they spoke had no significance. being alone and lonely has no dress code or language barrier. a limo picked her up from a location where most wouldn't want to live. the church was just a few miles away in a richer yet unstable part of town, until now. love found a way just one stop after...

pistachio nuts and vanilla ice cream...

ten years after my daughters' passing i reflected on some of the things while she was growing up. helping her with homework, tucking her in, and fixing her favorite snack on weekends just before bedtime. it was a strange combination of a small dish of pistachio nuts followed by a bowl of vanilla ice cream. "i love you daddy", were the last three words spoken. i put on the T V to watch a movie and then went to the bathroom for a minute. when i came back it was on a different channel as cartoons were being shown. maybe it was my imagination or i didn't have the proper channel to begin with. just out of habit i went to the kitchen and fixed a small dish of pistachio nuts followed by a bowl of vanilla ice cream. in the middle of the night i thought i heard a voice whisper in my hear "i love you daddy". a few red shells remained on the living room rug as the rest of the dish was empty. a spoon sat in the bowl that wasn't there before where the ice cream used to be....

a simple white dress...

a simple white dress sits in the closet of elizabeth jenkins. It's been there for seven years now as a reminder of what she wore the day her life was saved. she washes it every day trying to get the soot and smoke and blood stains out, then hangs it up to dry. its her way of removing the memory and the evil that took place in lower manhattan on September 11, 2,001. elizabeth jenkins was a receptionist three floors below from where the plane crashed into the south tower. on stairway b she walked down countless flights of stairs until she passed out from the overwhelming smoke. a firefighter carried her down 3 more flights and into one of the many ambulances waiting there outside. it was 15 minutes later that the south tower collapsed and her hero was gone in an instant. she never got to thank him and so she keeps cleaning a simple white dress to erase the stains of that day. the now 42 year old picked out a pink wedding gown for her first marriage to be. she wondered why just outside the dressing room a firefighter stood there and smiled at her and then suddenly disappeared. the pink wedding gown was no longer there, but instead a simple white dress....

beside her bedroom window...

she read his short story and paused for a moment as she re-read the last few sentences. his thoughts and feelings were absorbed in a moment when it was just for her. she could smell the single red rose which was not in the story, but between the lines of what had been written. there was a singing telegram delivered to her on a birthday that he remembered. she put the rose on her night stand beside her bedroom window. the doorbell woke her up at a time when it least was expected. "hello, its me...michael" he said with loving eyes. she knew the writer by screen name only but now felt that he was part of a dream which was time to share in real life. and so between the lines of a few sentences, a single red rose, and a happy birthday wish the two of them met for the first time. two heads now share the same pillow beside her bedroom window...

lost and found...

after the high school reunion i drove to the beach just a few a miles away. why not go all the way with those fond memories that we all hold dear to us. the smell of the salt water and the sound of the sea-gulls made me feel twenty years younger. under the boardwalk i laid with a blanket and stared up at the full moon. the incoming waves tickled my toes as the portable radio played some oldies. something below my right hand caught my *attention while it rested on the wet sand. i picked up the faded gold chain with two hearts attached just about two links apart. my first name and her first name was still engraved from twenty years ago. after the high school reunion she drove to a beach just a few miles away. she sat on a blanket not too far away from mine and looked at me with a familiar glance. my heart jumped to my throat and i could not speak a single word. all i could do was hold up an ankle bracelet. she dusted off the two hearts with her tears and put her arms around my neck as tight as they could hold. we missed each other at the reunion but in a way found the other when time and fate said it be so. the years gone by were never lost when a moment before it says hello again. a lesson to be learned under love, lost and found...*

a band-aid to go...

some people save their first earned dollar bill and put it in a plaque on the wall. for mary wilson it was the first band-aid that covered a scraped knee of her seven year old daughter. the three inch item just sat in the first page of a photo album beneath the cellophane. susan wilson was just another runaway at the age of thirteen which left mom with another cold case file seen on re-runs. in another state about a thousand miles away, the now 25 year old daughter fell down once again while running away from the abusive boyfriend she lived with. susan woke up on a plane heading home, hoping that mom would remember and forgive. she pressed down on the unknown band-aid on the same knee that was healed a long time ago. mom opened the door to let her in as she remembered and forgave at the same time. the three inch item which sat under the cellophane of the first page of a photo album was no longer there. you see, it was attached again where love heals all wounds from past to present....

one slice at a time...

the waitress looked exactly like her mother did some twenty years ago. could this be my daughter who i had never known about? my questions were carefully thought out and were asked with all due respect. she invited me back to her home and told me to talk about it with mom. the one night stand from so many years ago produced a child that never thought would see her biological dad. the three of us sat together and talked openly of mistakes and missed opportunities which now we all felt needed to be resolved. some tears were shed and hugs were exchanged in the form of a forgiveness that angels often smile upon from above. mom sliced the last part of a thanksgiving turkey as i picked up my knife and fork in gratitude. beneath a christmas tree sat a small black box that really couldn't be wrapped. our daughter stared at her mom with a smile, knowing already what was inside. the ring fit perfectly on her finger and so the engagement to be married the following year *became official. my daughter was the brides maid and watched me and mom cut the cake. we all laughed when she walked about the tables serving one slice at a time...*

an old hangout...

there was a place which was an old hangout from many years ago that had to be re-visited. it was a quiet bar with a cozy regular crowd. i sipped on my beer and sat on a stool that still remained. familiar faces had long since gone but memories remained the same. a jukebox with oldies sat in the corner and i played what i remembered. "that used to be my favorite tune" she said. her outfit was different and her hair looked somewhat new, yet those eyes and voice were the same. we remembered each other's name and how a slow dance was never forgotten. a car service drove us home that night to a place where it didn't really matter. we awoke on the same pillow and made love for the second time. i dusted off the box with an engagement ring that was saved just for her in case we ever met again. "yes, i will accept this", she said with tears in her eyes. the wedding album was perfect and the title on the cover described it as such. "an old hangout"....

as the war was over...

who knew that the war was officially over? for two soldiers on opposite sides it still raged on. a german fell asleep and the american had him in his sights with a finger on the trigger. i couldn't kill him while he slept so i just sat there next to him not knowing what to do. his open wallet lay there by his hand with a photo of him and his wife and two children. i opened mine and stared at a picture which had the same. "its time to go home", i said as i nudged him awake. we shared a smoke and talked about our families from each others photos. flyers dropped from the sky and both our radios transmitted that the war was finally over. we ended up in the same hospital and recovered from our wounds of battle and hate. it was thirty years later that we sat down at a table and ordered each others favorite meal. the four kids got along just fine as did our wives. and so the enemy wasn't much different from me as the war was over...

a third x-mas...

susan opened up moms x-mas gift and the seven year old held a new doll in her arms. she put it next to a doll from the previous x-mas who was dressed up as a soldier. mom cried to herself and knew how much her daughter missed daddy. it was three years ago that a letter came stating he was missing in action. "will daddy be coming soon"? she asked her mom. "i don't think so sweetheart, but just keep remembering him", mom replied. she tucked her daughter in and kissed her goodnight along with her two favorite dolls. the snow fell outside as she stared through the kitchen window which overlooked the front of her house. a few miles away a patient recovered from amnesia and was released from the hospital. he thought to himself "i'm not missing anymore and i have to get home". he could see a night light through the kitchen window as well as a x-mas tree that was missed for the last three years. mom awoke when the bell rang and she peeped through the keyhole of the front door. "hi hunny, i'm home", her husband said with a smile and a hundred tears. susan woke up and slowly walked into the kitchen where mom and dad stood hugging each other. dad held a late x-mas present out to his daughter. it was himself with outstretched arms. they sat around the tree for many years to come as two dolls in susan's room hugged each other at a time when it was needed the most....

her name is sara...

her name is sara and she is about 15 years old. i met her labor day weekend at a resort called daniels family resort in pennsylvania. her mom was standing at the bar in the outdoor poolside location when i just stared at her and didn't know why. later that evening the reason became clear as fate has its reasons for people getting together. i showed mom my first published book and she told me how her daughter loves to write and read. sara held my book and skimmed through the pages as she started to read. "i like this a lot", she said to me. mom purchased the book and that's where it all became a connection of sensitive and caring souls. sara bookmarked a few short stories for her mom to read and she did just that. the both of them cried in a few private moments. there was a hug from sara that made me feel wanted and accepted in her life. mom smiled and knew that her daughter was happy. we all checked out as our time was up and vacation was over. hopefully we will all get together again, you see love as not a trip but a final destination. her name is sara...

a hero times 40...

the sound of a four hundred pound food cart was heard rumbling down the isle just before his cell phone went dead. it was the first attempt to crash through a cockpit door where the terrorist pilot steered the plane towards his target of the Washington Capitol. it tilted right and then to the left as the passengers who fought back fell in the isle. this plane had room for 110 but on this particular morning it only seated 40. the last transmission from his wife told of how the Twin Towers were attacked and also the Pentagon. "You need to take control of the cockpit, they are using the planes as a suicide mission. do whatever it takes to stop them". the word spread through the 40 passengers and now a second attempt was made to ram the cockpit door. it killed the terrorist guard just outside as the pilot strapped himself in and tried to control the plane for its final target. the black box revealed its final moments with screaming and the words "take it down now" by the last fanatic. the crash site had military and police uniforms standing on each side of the road. four buses of friends and family slowly proceeded as they looked out their windows. outside they all stood at attention with a right hand face up against their forehead with a salute to honor them. you could see the tears streaming down each and every one of their faces. a farm in Pennsylvania was where they were laid to rest. the fourth target was never reached as it was only 15 minutes away. countless lives were saved from the bravery and determination of those aboard flight 93. a hero times 40....

PASSENGERS

Christian Adams

Todd Beamer, *32, was from Cranbury, New Jersey.*

Alan Beaven, *48, of Oakland, California, was an environmental lawyer.*

Mark Bingham, *31, of San Francisco owned a public relations firm, the Bingham group. He called his mother, Alice Hoglan, 15 minutes before the plane crashed and told her that the plane had been taken over by three men who claimed to have a bomb. Hoglan said her son told her that some passengers planned to try to regain control of the*

---

plane. "he said, 'I love you very, very much, ' "
Hoglan said.

Deora Bodley, 20, of Santa Clara, California,
was a university student.

Marion Britton

Thomas E. Burnett Jr., 38, of San Ramon,
California, was a senior vice president and chief
operating officer of Thoratec Corp., a medical
research and development company, and the
father of three. He made four calls to his wife,
Deena, from the plane. Deena Burnett said that
her husband told her that one passenger had been
stabbed and that "A group of us are going to do
something." He also told her that the people on
board knew about the attack on the world trade
center, apparently through other phone calls.

William Cashman

Georgine Corrigan

Joseph Deluca

Patrick Driscoll

Edward Felt, 41, was from Matawan, New
Jersey.

Colleen Fraser

Andrew Garcia

Jeremy Glick, *31, from West Milford, New Jersey, called his wife, Liz, and in-laws in New York on a cell phone to tell them the plane had been hijacked, Joanne Makely, Glick's mother-in-law, told CNN. Glick said that one of the hijackers "had a red box he said was a bomb, and one had a knife of some nature, Makely said. Glick asked Makely if the reports about the attacks on the World Trade Center were true, and she told him they were. He left the phone for a while, returning to say, "The men voted to attack the terrorists," Makely said.*

Lauren Grandcolas *of San Rafael, California, was a sales worker at Good Housekeeping Magazine.*

Donald F. Green, *52, was from Greenwich, Connecticut.*

Linda Gronlund

Richard Guadagno, *38, of Eureka, California, was the manager of the U.S. Fish and Wildlife Service's Humboldt Bay National Wildlife Refuge.*

Toshiya Kuge

Waleska Martinez

Nicole Miller

Mark Rothenberg

Christine Snyder, *32, was from Kailua, Hawaii. She was an arborist for the Outdoor Circle and was returning from a conference in Washington. She had been married less than a year.*

John Talignani

Honor Wainio

the sand box...

somewhere back in grade school at an age where love is innocent, we sat in the sandbox. just a small shovel to dig with and a pail to place the sand in. i drew a heart with our names in that area where no words were spoken but seen. she kissed me on the cheek and that was where it all started. her name and face were embedded in my mind even though it was now twenty five years later. it was like a trivia question that the mind asked the heart. with no thoughts of this past event, i sat on a beach and stared at the incoming waves. a sea shell whispered in my ear my name being called by her once again. a young girl about the same age as me sat on the sand not too far away. she stared out at the incoming waves and held a sea shell to her ear. our footprints walked closer and we both lay down our blankets to share with each other. her finger drew a heart in the sand with our names in that area where no words were spoken but seen....

send in the clowns...

i already phoned the hospital to let them know i would arrive in a clowns outfit. they understood my explanation of how my daughter just loved them with each visit to the circus and that this would be a pleasant surprise. "hello mr. reisman, we've been expecting you and we hope this brings a smile to your daughters face.". the receptionist cried to herself as she noticed the love beneath my make-up. i peeked into her room as she lay there with the tubes and other hospital gadgets attached to her body. she tilted her head towards me and opened one eye. i honked on my plastic horn and sprinkled confetti at the foot of her bed. the other eye opened and she smiled and laughed with an outstretched arm. maybe she thought that the circus had come to visit her. i told a few jokes to my eleven year old as she held my hand and grinned with her weakened lips. my thirty minutes was up as visiting hours were now over. the nurse motioned me towards the door as she put her finger on her lips, a gesture to be quiet as i left. "daddy, is that you"? a hoarse whisper said. the nurse gave me another me another five minutes to say goodbye. "you were always my favorite clown daddy, i just want you to know that. there is an angel here now that wants to take me home, i love you daddy." the green wave lines on the monitor went flat as some heavy tears washed away my make-up. the nurse put her hand on my shoulder and we walked back to the empty elevator. the circus came to town and i sat in same seat i did before. the box of popcorn slightly tilted as a little unseen hand shared a snack with her favorite clown.... in memory of Stephanie Reisman, my Angel daughter

a favorite table...

the club was still there even though the name has changed. the people and music were different but my old favorite table still remained. an old jukebox was replaced by a live band and i sat at my table and thought back to some old memories. a lady sat next to me and said "don't you just hate this new stuff"? i nodded my head yes as i sipped on my fourth beer. she pointed to an ankle chain that she wore and said "remember me"? "is that you carol"? i said with a look of surprise and delight. the lights went dim and the live band was no longer there, just a jukebox and a memory. she slipped in a quarter and played unchained melody by the righteous brothers. it was a slow dance continued as if we never left the place. the live band at our wedding held up a quarter and played our favorite song...

Todd Beamer, 32, was from Cranbury, New Jersey...

UNITED AIRLINES FLIGHT 93... i felt the urge to write this story but not from my own eyes. it seemed another force guided my fingers for this detailed event in a few final moments. Todd Beamer took over and so this is his account..."we heard from our cell phones that two of the towers in N.Y were attacked by terrorists and that the Pentagon was also hit. a suicide bomber stood in front of the cockpit with his finger on a detonation device strapped to his chest. i knew that this was just a ploy to keep us in our seats. i told the other passengers that this plane was a target bent on destroying another building. we re-grouped and thought out a plan of action. we grabbed all available cans of soda and everything else we could get our hands on as a weapon. four of us charged the entrance to the cockpit and killed the terrorist in our way. we used a cart and rammed the cockpit door until it finally broke down. there was a passenger who had some flying hours as a pilot and said "if the plane is not too low, then maybe i can bring it back up to a safe altitude." i punched and kicked the terrorist until he fell down and choked him with my bare hands. in his last dying breath he shouted "take it down, take it down". the pilot strapped in his seatbelt as the plane descended. my hands were around his neck but the grip on the steering wheel was too firm. plane four never reached its target as it went down and crashed in a farm in Pennsylvania. i awoke in a sweat the next day and published this article. Todd Beamer, 32, was from Cranbury, New Jersey...

as she sits and waits...

the routine changed slightly as i took the staircase down four flights instead of riding the elevator. it was from my girlfriends apartment complex that i left on a usual saturday night to travel back home. the year was 1972 and it was about eleven o'clock that summer evening when the streets were quiet as the same route i had traveled before was so very familiar. there was my green light just under an overpass on ave s where macdonald avenue crossed this intersection. i never saw the other car speeding under the overpass from my right side. a thunderous crash deafened my ears for a moment as my car spun around twice. it was in slow motion that my glasses left my face while my two hands held tightly to the steering wheel. a warm embrace engulfed my entire being as the car spun over 200 feet and hit a parked car on the opposite side of the intersection. not a scratch nor a bruise as my car was crushed in from the passenger side to just within inches of where I sat. i look back now and think of the fate of how it all happened. the difference in time from taking the staircase as opposed to the elevator had that event occur. in our lives these things happen without us knowing. yet somewhere an angel does as she sits and waits and hugs us...

the chat...

Patricia says:
hi sweetie
michael says:
hi hun
Patricia says:
how was your day
michael says:
only 14 mails today, weird. thats an all time low
Patricia says:
i have 285 want some
michael says:
no thanx
michael says:
lol
Patricia says:
lol
michael says:
any luck at the library?
Patricia says:
bambi wasn't in i left her a message
michael says:
ok
michael winks:

Play "Knock"

Patricia winks:

Play "Heart"
michael winks:

Play "Heart"
Patricia says:
thanks
michael says:
the perfect opening for our chat
Patricia says:
yes
michael says:
i got aol opened now so i can see the weather. its
68 now
Patricia says:
it's 61 here
michael says:
close
Patricia says:
yes
Patricia says:
did you watch paranormal state last night
michael says:
i taped it and watched it today
Patricia says:
i watched it last night
michael says:
i go to bed between 8 and 830
Patricia says:
that's early
michael says:

yes, i start my beer drinking between 3 and 330.
so by 8pm im ready to eat and then sleep
michael winks:

Play "Bouncy Ball"
Patricia says:
i see a regular routine
michael says:
yes
michael says:
love you
Patricia says:
love you too
michael says:
i am completely baffled at what you are trying
to research. something about power tools?
Patricia says:
yes for my class in strategic management i work
for a power tool company
michael says:
and what is it exactly about power tools you
need to know?
Patricia says:
the key economic indexes
Patricia says:
it's in the us census but i can't find it
michael says:
so its "key economic indexes of power tools"?
Patricia says:
i already tried that it brings me to a page that
has the answer for sale and i can't do that i'll fail
michael says:

i see
Patricia says:
the census has all kinds of ways to find power
tools just not what i need
michael says:
http://www.brainmass.com/homework-help/
business/business-analysis/133891
Patricia says:
that's the one i can't use
michael says:
bummer hun
michael says:
i tried
Patricia says:
i know
michael says:
hold on a sec....
michael says:
http://www.associatedcontent.com/
*article/381880/the_power_tool_industry_and_*
economic.html
Patricia says:
i can try it let me write it down
michael says:
ok
michael says:
its a link, just click on it and it will take you to
the web site
Patricia says:
okay i'll try that
Patricia says:
thank you sweetie

michael says:
welcome my hunny bunny
michael winks:

Play "Frog"
Patricia says:
i collect frogs you know
michael says:
yes
Patricia says:
i still like this one the best
Patricia winks:

Play "Heart"
michael says:
me too
michael says:
beer 3, brb...
michael says:
cheers
Patricia says:
cheers sweetie
michael says:
liberty tonite at 730
Patricia says:
have fun
michael says:
ill wathc an hour then record the rest
Patricia says:
i'm happy you get to see your women play
michael says:
yes, good thing i got the MSG channel

Patricia says:
do you watch anything else on there
michael says:
sometimes they have special programs on the
giants
Patricia says:
do they show the concerts or the boxing that
they have there
michael says:
yes, all of that
Patricia says:
wow
michael says:
under my pillow i got the channel P.A.T.T.I. thats
when i tune you into my dreams
Patricia says:
i like that maybe we have the same dreams some
nights
michael says:
most likely for sure hun
michael winks:

Play "UFO"
Patricia says:
i like that little guy
michael says:
cool ufo greeting
Patricia says:
yup
michael says:
pretty snow scene wallpaper today
Patricia says:

yes it was i sent you a note
michael says:
i read it, thanx
michael says:
smooch
Patricia says:
smooch
michael says:
i added some more stories last night to the word
documnent from gather
Patricia says:
good a few at a time and you'll be done before
you know it.
michael says:
yes. its a slow process. i have gather open and
word at the same time. then you have copy and
paste
Patricia says:
yes i've done projects like that before
michael says:
so u know what its like
Patricia says:
yes it's a pain in the butt
michael says:
sure is
michael says:
wed nights at 9 or 10 or both are episodes of the
new twighlight zone tv series
Patricia says:
what channel
michael says:
ch 9

Patricia says:
abc cbs nbc fox
michael says:
ch 9 is WOR over here
Patricia says:
ch 9 is cbs here
michael says:
or my 9
Patricia says:
i don't get wor
michael says:
well u got ch 9
Patricia says:
yes i do
michael says:
good, make a note to watch or record it
Patricia says:
i can't record it i don't have a dvr they don't have
them up here yet
michael says:
what about a VCR tape recorder?
Patricia says:
no just a dvd player
michael says:
i see
Patricia says:
my vcr bit the dust and i never replaced it
michael says:
pork fried rice last night with 2 packets of
chinese mustard
Patricia says:
i love pork fried rice and i like chinese mustard

michael says:
more in common my hunny bunny
Patricia says:
you said it sweetie
Patricia says:
i took my sister home from the hospital today
and took her to the store so i have cottage cheese
now
michael says:
good deal
michael says:
u gonna love it on the pasta dish
Patricia says:
i have to make the pasta dish first
michael says:
yes
Patricia says:
tomorrow
michael says:
let it sit in fridge overnight. it taste better the
next day as it solidifies
Patricia says:
okay i'll do it
michael says:
then use microwave or put in frying pan and
stir it with a little cooking oil
Patricia says:
yes dear
michael says:
<<<your favorite writer and cook
Patricia says:
my favorite everything

michael says:
thats why we love each other
Patricia says:
yes it is
michael says:
when we chat here, its almost like we are
together
Patricia says:
yes i feel like you're sitting next to me
michael says:
there ya go
michael says:
just what i was thinking hun
Patricia says:
was i reading your mind or were you reading
mine
michael says:
the thought enters at the same time
Patricia says:
that's probably so
michael says:
its just a matter of who types what first
Patricia says:
true, very true
michael winks:

Play "Dancer"

Patricia just sent you a nudge.

You have just sent a nudge.

michael says:
we are soooooo good together
Patricia says:
i'm afraid of what will happen if we ever
actually meet
michael says:
eyes, then arms with hug, then "THE KISS"
Patricia says:
yes that will be wonderful
michael says:
i guess we were both just daydreaming about
that
Patricia says:
yes it was great

to be found...

the crickets rubbed their legs together and made music in the night. some fireflies lit up the lawn as a frog croaked its bedtime story. these memories had me visit a hotel i once stayed at as a kid. eventually we all go back to a place we held that special. my parents had long since been gone where they once drove us all to in the years and summer months of memories that had to be re-visited. it was october and the hotel was closed so there was no need to check in. i zipped up my sweatshirt in the chill of the air that was once warm. there was a campfire in the distance where we used to sit around and i walked slowly towards it. she sat there still and quiet, a childhood memory of a first love. then the sound of footsteps behind me. it was a place her parents took her as a child many years ago where she wanted to hear the crickets again, to see the fireflies, and hear a frog croak a bedtime story. the october chill suddenly left the air as it became warm once again. the lawn lit up and again we heard some music in the night. michael and patricia re-introduced themselves in a place where time had no meaning. you can visit this hotel anytime of year and if you look carefully, there may be a zipped up sweatshirt to be found...

B4...

it took place at an after hours club just up two flights of stairs. word of mouth only knew about it as it was an illegal bar. the same faces stared down at their drinks in a lonely desperation of meeting mister or miss right. nobody saw the sunlight through the blackened out painted windows at 6am that morning. i stood over the jukebox with a quarter in my hand and pushed the button that read B4. it was an oldie song called "sometimes when we touch", by Dan Hill. "wanna dance"? a familiar face from the bar said. "sure, why not? i replied. we introduced ourselves with a slurred speech that often was forgotten. the last thing i remembered was exchanging phone numbers from two fresh napkins that sat on the bar. i called her the following friday as i drove to her apartment about ten miles away. my finger hit the doorbell just below apartment number B4. strange coincidence huh? we talked while sober for the first time and got to know each other. then we made love and dated for the whole following year. before and after was the name of the wedding chapel that performed our ceremony. the live band had a drummer which displayed the name of their group on the front of his bass drum. it read B4....

my lady...

and so there is no logic or reason for what i am about to write, therefore my heart will explain itself in just a matter of feelings. her name will not be mentioned so i will refer to her as "my lady". she lives in another state and we chat sometimes on the computer and even talk on the phone. how can you love somebody you have never met? well in my dreams i see her often and maybe that is the reality that science can't put their finger on. our status whether it be married or single is not important here, for that makes a simple feeling on both our parts a complicated issue in the eyes of the general public and of course the media. nobody knows what day by day events bring, so let the future take its course. somewhere in michigan i stopped off at a flower shop. a red rose stood on display that i had seen in a dream before. i placed it on her pillow while she slept. it was for "my lady"...

upstairs...

it was so strange how they met that i had to write a story about them. it all began in two separate locations as their mail introduced each other on the computer. they shared each others picture and talked about things in common. their screen names were added to each others buddy list and the live chat began. no mention of where each other lived, for it was assumed that each was at least a city or state apart, like 95% of all those who meet online. we walked our dogs the same time every morning but never noticed each other before. across the street was a park and our dogs sniffed each other as dogs often do. "how did you get here"? i said with a confused look on my face. she replied " i live in the complex just behind us across the street from this park". needless to say, we both laughed out loud and hugged and kissed at our first true meeting in person. she giggled when i asked her if i could walk her home. the dogs were now friends also and maybe that was a good sign. back in the apartment complex she pointed to where she lived. it was the same address as mine and we both nearly flipped out. she was a neighbor of mine who lived directly above on the second floor of our condo. "hey, think we can get together sometime"? she said. "let me call a cab or find a train or book a flight and then i'll let you know" i replied. we both burst into laughter as she invited me upstairs....

jennifer...

her seeing eye dog was distracted for a moment by a cat that ran across the street. the light changed to green for the cars to the left and right of her on this dark and foggy night. i raced to the middle of the road and pulled her to the sidewalk as the traffic raced by. the dog stopped barking and i put his leash back in her hand. jennifer was born blind and got through life which almost was taken away a few moments ago. she asked who i was and i told her my name as we walked together and talked on her way home. "thank you my kind stranger for what you did tonight", she said as we approached her front door. the dog licked my hand when i petted him a goodbye for now. she touched my face with her fingers and said "now i know what you look like". "goodnight jennifer", i said and walked back to my car and drove home. it was maybe a month later when i returned and rang her doorbell. "hi, its me michael, remember? the dog sniffed my leg then licked my hand again. "please come in" she said. her hands touched my face and she said "oh, you're growing a beard now"? we both laughed and sat together on the couch in her living room. her dog rested one paw on my foot as if it was a welcome home greeting. we started dating and after one year it became x-mas eve. i opened my gift to find a beard trimmer which she knew i needed to have. her present was only maybe an inch long and deep as she wondered what was so small a gift. jennifer took out the engagement ring and i placed it on her finger. the dog sat up and barked as he licked both our hands. six months later she became a june bride and we kissed for the first time. i prayed for long before that event that she could see me. maybe it was an angel on top of our tree, who knows? but jennifer's eyes became clear and focused as a miracle happened. her seeing eye dog was no longer that, just a pet dog now who no longer needed a leash. he sniffed my leg and licked my hand just before he climbed into bed with us. this story is verified to be true by what you believe in...

holding hands...

in the school yard we slid down the sliding pond and held hands. across two desks just before the exam in grammar school we did the same, wishing each other good luck. there was a class photo taken at our graduation but it never showed us below the waist as we held hands. remember the footprints on the beach as we raced into the waves together? we sat in the front seat of my car watching a drive in movie and held hands. there was an office we worked together and you were the new employee. i led you to the water cooler, remember? there was a circle dance and you were my partner to the right side as we held hands. dad marched you down the isle and we stood before the priest. the best man handed me a ring and i placed it on your finger. we said our vows as we held hands. a new born son could be seen behind the glass of the delivery room. i smiled and watched you and him holding hands. remember?

of a hat and a tie...

the locals stared at the stranger who entered their bar with a shirt and tie and funny shoes. the waitress served him a cold beer and winked the only friendly smile that was to be seen. she placed her cowboy hat on his head and said "make yourself at home stranger". after the fourth drink he loosened up and the once hostile crowd laughed as he took off his funny shoes. michael danced with the waitress when she was on a break and joined him for a short chat at his table. she put on his tie as the midwest and northeast somehow became connected. they danced slow and fast and kicked up the saw dust on the wooden texas floor. jodie said goodbye after a week of his short visit as he returned her hat and she returned his tie. michael packed his belongings and his car drove out of the motel lot as he made it to the main road. the entrance to the highway had a hitchhiker standing there with her thumb out and a suitcase by her feet. he pulled over and kissed jodie with the passion and love that was empty in both their lives. the ride back to new york had a reservation for the midwest girl and the northeast guy. the wedding floor was wooden with some sawdust as he wore her cowboy hat and she wore his tie...

for the last ten years...

how did this hitch hiker end up down the road five miles away from last i saw him? i stopped the car to give him a ride and find out why. the young man sort of looked like me only ten years younger which gave me an eerie feeling. "where you headed to young man"?, i said. "to a church not too far from here. i'm supposed to get married you see", he replied. i looked in the rear view mirror and noticed his old ragged outfit was now a tuxedo. "you some sort of magician or something. how did you change like that?" i asked. "wanna see my bride to be"? he handed me a photo which shook me up so much, i had to pull over and get out of the car. it was the same girl i was supposed to marry ten years ago. "ever wonder why you keep driving down these same roads"? he asked. i thought about it for a while and did in fact wonder why. "its time to go home now. you are me back then and just didn't realize you crashed into a tree and died. and so we drove towards the horizon where a bright white light was waiting. an old self and a new self met where things had to be settled for a final time. the church was just up ahead as i parked the car. the wedding plans were now in front me where my bride was waiting for the last ten years...

from where she lived...

she held the newborn son in her arms, he was 8lbs 22ounces. the year was 1981 during the summer at a hospital not too far away from where she lived. the father was not known and mom raised the little boy by herself the best she could. his birthmark was barely noticeable but it grew along with him, a cleft on his little chin. tommy got on the school bus and the driver closed the door as they all rode to school a few miles away. there was a knock on moms door xmas eve as a man with a uniform stood outside. "my bus broke down, may i come in and use your phone please"? little tommy stared at him as so did the mother. "can we talk"? he said to her. he described some events that happened in 1980 which shook her into recognition of a one night stand. as he spoke she noticed a cleft on his chin and the same color eyes as her little boy. the bus driver put a present under the tree and tommy opened it. a yellow toy school bus with a note for mom was attached. it read..."i knew he was my son the first time he got on the bus. please forgive me for showing up too many years later". mom cried, but it was tears of joy that were shed. she introduced him to their son and explained that dad was a long trip away from home, but has now returned. tommy hugged the man in uniform and asked dad to tuck him in. the marriage was set to take place soon after in a church not too far away from where she lived...

between man and beast...

a typical night in a department store became something more than that for henry watson. he had forgotten to take his blood pressure pills the day before and felt suddenly dizzy. it was fifteen minutes before closing time when henry blacked out in the men's room on the first floor. he awoke and looked at his watch which read 11pm. the store had already been closed for two hours. the lights were out except for a few florescent bulbs which served as a security precaution. he made his way to the main exit but the iron gate was shut down tight. it would be another nine hours before the store would re-open. he reached into his pocket and swallowed a pill which he had forgotten before. not too far behind him he heard the barking of a dog and then a growl. it was a 200 pound german shepherd guard dog that protected the store from intruders. henry ran to the shut down escalator with the dog in hot pursuit. it gnawed into his left pants leg and he screamed out in pain. he raced to a bathroom on the second floor and shut the door behind him. blood ran down his leg and he pulled off his tie and made a tourniquet around the open wound. 6 hours in the bathroom he wondered what to do next until the store would open in 3 more hours. he peaked out of the door to see a sign by the escalator which read "sports department third floor". it was quiet outside the bathroom except for the sound of paws walking on the third floor. henry sprinted up the *escalator with one leg limping along the way. a display of a bow and arrows caught his eye and he broke the glass as the mad and growling dog stared at him from about twenty feet away. henry set the arrow in the bow and knew he had only one shot to take. the morning crowd filed into the department store and shortly after an ambulance arrived. henry woke up in a hospital bed from loss of blood and a state of shock. the dog that attacked him was wounded by an arrow in his left leg, but also survived. this german shepherd was placed in a shelter and henry adopted him unknown that it was the same dog who attacked him. the german shepherd licked and kissed an old wound on his left leg from a year before. harry noticed a limp in his pets left paw and he held it in his hands. forgiveness with love and compassion was exchanged between man and beast...*

the tree house...

maybe it was a coincidence or fate, i'm not really sure which it was. however i ended up moving back to an old neighborhood on the same exact block i used to live on over thirty years ago. the deal went smoothly and the property was now mine. the numbers 1106 were still on the front door and all my new furniture was moved in. i painted and set up the house just the way i remembered it to be. down the steps of the basement and to the right was a door that led to the backyard i used to play in. the tree house was still there that dad built for me so many years ago. i stared at the small ladder and had flashbacks of a specific childhood memory. it was there that i invited the girl next door to climb with me as we played house. her face was as clear as the moment of our first kiss. i climbed the ladder and sat there for a moment. a voice from below said "michael, is that you"? a neighbor who had never moved and still lived next door climbed up and sat beside me. it was then that we had our second kiss. she moved in with me and we soon got married. our son climbed a ladder and sat in the tree house that i had rebuilt for him. he invited a new girl neighbor from next door as they shared a first kiss...

a second chance...

i had to go back to the old neighborhood where i grew up. it was those memories where the intensity of my nightly dreams made me do so. the grammar school, the high school, the college was still there as each was visited. a parking lot which used to have a drive in movie was now replaced by a shopping mall. i fell asleep while daydreaming of events some thirty years ago. a tap on my drivers side window had a waitress saying "here is your burger and fries with two large cokes". i rolled down the window and sat it on the seat in front of me. she had to go back to the old neighborhood where she grew up and sat beside me in a car that i used to drive. me and an old high school sweetheart talked of old times and what we planned for the future. we visited the shopping mall and bought some new clothes for our 10 year old daughter and 13 year old son. maybe time and memories connect as they allow us a second chance....

they never wilted away...

i shut the television off with the remote control by my bedside. the hospital room was silent except for a few footsteps heard out in the hall. my hand reached for the phone as i spoke to the florist on the other end. the next day my girlfriend received a dozen roses along with a card. she was out of state at the time when the delivery was made. the card read..."for the twelve years i have known you, these roses are for each one. love, Michael. she came back from her business trip and entered the hospital. the receptionist looked up the name that was requested. I'm sorry miss, but that patient passed away last night". a fresh dozen roses that she held in her hands was watered by tears from her eyes. she placed them in a vase on a nightstand in her bedroom which eventually wilted away. the weeks and months passed by which seemed like years in the mourning of her beloved boyfriend. there was a knock on her door one morning as the delivery boy stood there with a dozen roses and a card attached. it read "for the 15 years i have known you these roses are for each one". 3 extra roses were enclosed in the cellophane wrapping. she smiled and sat them in a vase on

her nightstand in her bedroom. they never wilted
away....

romantic eyes...

our agent booked us for a gig at a sweet sixteen
party. luckily it was in the same borough so we
didn't have to travel that far. the young girl of
honor stared at me while we played our tunes
and i looked back at her with the same romantic
eyes. during a 20 minute break we sat at her table
and talked. at the time i was 20 and she was 16.
her mom and dad seemed to like me and after
the party was over i was invited to her home the
following weekend. we dated for 4 years and then
she moved out of state to a college of her choice.
it was then that we lost contact with each other.
our manager booked us at a gig out of state some
10 years later. it was worth the drive as the event
was huge and the pay was great. Somebody's
wedding anniversary in a huge hall with over 300
guests. mom and dad celebrated as their 26 year
old daughter stared at a 30 year old drummer.
that same romantic look never left us and we
danced together during a 20 minute break. our
band split up but still kept in touch. they attended
our wedding a few months later as i sat in on a
special song with some old drumsticks that were
saved. the bride stared at the groom and he stared
back with the same romantic eyes...

round trip...

i looked back down from above as a doctor put something on my chest, then yelled "clear". not wanting to go back, i looked a little more above and then entered a tunnel of sorts. before i reached the light at the end, there were old friends, neighbors, relatives, and pets that greeted me along the way. there was a book that was to be signed at the entrance of a garden and then i was led away to some classroom which seemed to be that of orientation. lessons learned and others still needed were shown to the class along with certain rules on how and what to do here. there were portals shown to me where one may cross through back to the earth plane if one wished to visit. there were libraries, museums, entertainment, and a lot of what i remembered back on earth. the soul appeared as we wanted it to be at any age and may be recognized by others who once knew us. there were zoos with no cages as we and the animals mingled and spoke together in comfort with love and without fear. an old familiar job was offered to me as mail carrier and a writer. everything was clearer and transportation was just a thought away. i was led away after what seemed to be a few months to the garden which i first entered. an angel told me to sign out and gave me a pen. "i don't want to go back", i said. "it is not your time", he replied. just a visit. i looked below me and suddenly was pulled down as i heard a doctor yell "clear". when i awoke they explained to me i was gone for 7 minutes. maybe there were a few more lessons to be learned...😇

crayons and a coloring book...

i filled out a page in my coloring book with bright colored crayons. it had the sun and moon painted with a blue line connecting the two. above each was our names. the page was ripped out and i handed it to her just before our 5th grade class ended. she saw it and responded with a page of her own. there were two stick figures outside a church which to me represented a marriage of sorts. amazing how young love is so pure and innocent. thirty years later i sat in a restaurant and ordered my food. the waitress came up to me for a second time and handed me a box of crayons as she smiled. i scribbled on the napkin how much i missed and loved her. two human people who once were stick figures stood outside of a church with the sun and moon already connected by the blue line that held them together. our invitations had long been printed so many years ago with crayons and a coloring book...

the antique shop...

the antique shop was empty except for me and the old man behind the counter. "take your time son and browse around", he said while dusting off the cash register. a porcelain angel caught my eye that sat in a glass case. "ill need to unlock that before you can get a good look at her", he said. "she's very rare and one of a kind you see. my most expensive and protected possession." there was something about her sad eyes that drew me to her and the old man let me hold her in my hands. he slipped the credit card through his scanner and the purchase was complete for 750 dollars. i took her home and placed the item in a closed glass curio cabinet in my living room. there were no signatures of the author nor a date or place from where it was made. a strange coincidence occurred to my thinking that the price of 750 was also my address, 750 hill side ave. her sad eyes suddenly looked happy and there was a smile on her face that wasn't there before. i guess she saw the same in mine. the doorbell rang new years eve and i invited the stranger in. her wings hugged me and her smile became a kiss. if you pass the antique shop on your way home, make sure to look around. ask the old man if he has a key to unlock something very rare and one of a kind...

on the 25th floor...

maria pushed the cart through the isles of the office on the 25th floor. coffee, bagels, and other items were sold on a daily basis. she handed me a bagel and cream cheese and a large coffee with extra sugar. she spoke english but not too well, just enough to understand what she was saying. one morning i layed a rose on her cart as she picked it up and smelled something other than breakfast.

there was a difference in our ages and culture but that was soon settled by a smile that was universal in nature. she accepted my offer as a secretary to the vice president in charge of promotion and production. a cart was wheeled in on the 25th floor some months later. it had a wedding cake with a bride and groom sitting at the top. love finds a way in all ages and backgrounds on floors where a rose says it all. a lesson for those concerned who happen to get off on the 25th floor....

trying to get home...

there were some winding country roads in pennsylvania that i traveled some years back. to my recollection i will relate to you the events on that evening and the following days...a light rain was swept away by the windshield wipers when a young girl stood in the road just around a curve. her thumb was up trying to hitch a ride. there was blood dripping from her forehead and i stopped the car to help. she looked about 13 or 14 holding a knapsack filled with books. then she collapsed by the side of the road and i carried her into the backseat of my car. i wrapped a handkerchief around her forehead and drove ahead looking for some help. she pointed to a dirt road that led off to the right where i could see a farmhouse in the distance. "i'm just trying to get home" she said with a weakened smile. i pulled up to the house and a front porch light turned on. i got out of the car and opened the rear door but nobody was there, she just disappeared. an elderly couple came out to greet me and said "come inside my dear stranger, there are some things you need to know about what just happened". "you are not the first person who came here with our daughter. you see, she was killed by a driver some fifteen years ago while walking home from school. we believe she doesn't know what happened and is still trying to come home". i couldn't absorb the events of that night as reality and drove back home in a semi state of shock. when i reached my hometown of new york, i pulled into a car wash just a few blocks from where i lived. after the car was washed and vacuumed an attendant approached me and said " should i throw out this bloodied handkerchief i found in your back seat?" ....

the 5th reel...

janet holiday sat in her bedroom and watched some old black and white movies. she was 86 and a big Hollywood star back in the late 1930's through the early 1940's. romantic films were her style with the top leading male actors of her time. there were a few romantic flings but nothing permanent to speak of. her long time butler shut off the movie and gave her medicine as he watched her go to sleep. janet holiday was a lonely soul looking and living in the past for her true love. he put away her favorite four reels and shut the projector off. she died in her sleep from natural causes as the butler packed up her belongings. in the middle of the night he heard voices coming from her bedroom. an old black and white film was playing on the white screen that he thought was taken down earlier. he watched Janet Holiday stand before a doorway pleading for him not to leave. the butler in the movie returned and kissed her passionately as he promised to marry her. it was on a 5th reel that was never made before. she was happy now and the butler was never was found again for it was only the 5th reel that is left for those who need it.

next stop crestwood...

the hustle and bustle of everyday life along with a failing marriage had henry at his wits end. on his way home he stared out the trains window and dreamed of a simpler place in time. "next stop crestwood" the conductor yelled, but it wasn't there before. he could see some ladies walking around with a parasol and a bonnet with frilly long extending gowns. it looked like a scene from the late 1800's. he awoke to his usual stop and the wife nagged him with a call from his boss threatening to fire him. divorce was scheduled and a custody battle made life almost unbearable for henry. "next stop crestwood", the conductor yelled as this time he stayed awake and got off of the train. a young lady greeted him with a bonnet and a parasol with a long extended gown. they held hands and walked off together in a simpler and happier time. henry's wife worried that evening when he didn't come home from work. it seemed a man jumped from a train in between station stops and was found dead on the tracks. an ambulance took the body away which on the back could be read "crestwood emergency service vehicle". henry now lives in a place where time was waiting just for him....

without a net...

the lights dimmed under the big top and all that was heard was a drum roll below. two spot lights shown above on barry and belinda, each on their own platform about fifty feet apart and two hundred feet above the floor below. for the first time ever she would perform a triple summersault and he would attempt to catch her without a net below. the drum roll became silent and barry adjusted his wristbands while putting the white chalk on each palm to prevent sweating. his legs hung over the crossbar and he did his first swing. belinda would swing three times to gain height just before she would release and summersault three times in mid-air before the catch could be made. only one of her hands met its mark as he desperately tried to grab the other. their palms lost touch and belinda fell two hundred feet below without a net. the lights came back on and the crowd moaned and cried as belinda lay motionless. barry prayed from his platform and time seemed to stand still for a moment. then a net was raised as she did her triple once again back in time. he caught her as the

crowd stood on their feet and applauded. somehow
a prayer was answered without question as love
does have its miracles. there was a drum roll at
their wedding without a net...

the bus stop...

it started to rain at the bus stop and i held my
umbrella over the head of a young lady in front
me. she turned around and smiled for the simple
gesture. she must have lost her money as she
scrambled through her purse, so i paid her fare
and she was grateful. the young lady waved at
me from the sidewalk as i looked out the window
and waved back with a smile after she got off at
her stop. a few months later we met again as i was
on my way to a job interview. this time we got
off together and happened to walk into the same
building. how crazy was this? i thought as both of
us got off at the same floor and entered the same
company of my interview. she disappeared along
a hallway and i waited in the reception area to be
called. the young lady sat across from me with
a smile as we talked about my qualifications for
the new job. she laughed a compassionate giggle
and then put an umbrella over my head and said
"you're hired"! we met every morning at a bus
stop and became somewhat intimate after dating
for the next 2 years. she paid my fare on a bus to
atlantic city on our way to the honeymoon....

1981...

two people met online and stared at each others photo from their profile. it also showed up in the instant message screen where they finally got together and chatted for the first time. so michigan and new york was a distance only in geography, but not in the feelings they felt for each other. after a few weeks and months the phone calls brought them even closer together. one phone conversation had him ask her about the photo she displayed. "well, that was my favorite and i thought it looked the best from 1981." he replied, "your not going to believe this, but so is mine". it was strange and beyond a coincidence that the same year of each of their photos were selected. they talked and found out about their age at the present time. he was 61 and she was 59. diana ross and lionel ritchie sang "endless love" in a place where oldies had two people dance for the first time. "you look so familiar to me" they both said to each other. so where does time and love begin and end again? maybe an angel knows who places those in a spot where it all began.

a writers dream... ((sara))

she was beyond her years of 15 with the maturity of a thirty year old. he was just a kid at heart who thought and felt like a teenager at the age of 61. a chance meeting at a resort had the two of them meet for the first time. michael met her mom at poolside and told her about his first published book. she looked at the title and read the back cover. "this looks really interesting, may i buy a copy from you"? she said. his book was sold right there on the spot. "my daughter loves to read and as a matter of fact she loves to write, i think she will enjoy your book.". it was that weekend that i then met sara. in the lounge we sat and talked as sara just loved the first few stories. she even book-marked a few for her mom to read. we talked of things in common and even about subjects of reincarnation, soul mates, and topics that only two old souls would know about. a bond was established which rarely happens between two strangers as some hugs were exchanged as if they had done so before. it was a beautiful weekend as I had met a beautiful soul. my writings inspired her as sara wrote with the passion and creativity that could only come from the heart. i recently got mail from sara which said, "i miss you too, and mom says hello. my english teacher reads one story a day in class to the rest of us". that mail left a lump in my throat knowing that one and so many others have been touched in a very special way. sara went on to write her first book which was titled "my hero". it was a true story about a writer who inspired her over a weekend at a resort some summers ago. it made the best seller list and mom gave her a hug which I often do in my dreams. michael and sara sat together behind a table at a famous book store where people stood on a long line waiting for their autographs...

the open window...

the babysitter opened a window in the two year olds room to let in some air. it was a hot july summer evening when she went back to the living room and put a pair of head phones over her ears and continued to do her homework. little rebecca climbed out of the open window onto the fire escape and looked down from ten stories above. i was just coming home when the cries of my baby had me look up. the babysitter took off her head phones and heard the same crying from outside the bedroom window. my finger pushed the button in the elevator as i repeatedly hit the number 10, hoping it would get me there in time. she crawled out the open window and grabbed the child just before my daughter was about to fall, but lost her grip. i raced into the apartment as the baby sitter sat there on the fire escape shaken and hysterically crying. the dream was so real that it left me in tears and wondered if this was an event to come. it was late june that the nightmare occurred and i decided to install an air-conditioner in my daughters room the following day. i hired a babysitter in july feeling comfortable now that the window was shut leading to the fire escape. a blackout occurred and she opened the other window to let some air into my daughters bedroom....

Michael Reisman

merry-go-round...

coney island, brooklyn n.y. it's been around for as long as we can remember. for those who haven't been there, let me take you on a tour...the rides range from a speedy roller coaster to a slow ride through the tunnel of love. hot buttered popcorn and pink cotton candy fill the air along with nathan's famous burgers and fries. the scent of the waves can be smelled under the boardwalk crashing over the sand below. for me the painted horses on the merry-go-round have a special meaning. it was there that a twelve year old boy and an a ten year old girl shared a ride on the same horse. i had to go back there to re-capture a dream of a first love. it was forty years later when i sat on those same painted horses as it rode up and down like it always did before. a lady sat behind me and asked "you been here before"? i turned my head around to see an older face but the same young eyes that i stared into with a loving glance. we shared some rides once again and left together with some famous fries and burgers from nathan's. our kids now grown come back to where mom and dad first met. they both sat on a merry-go-round and looked behind them....

a library, a silent kiss...

it was in a public library in one of the isles where it all began. two hands reached for the same book on a shelf in the romance section. we both *laughed and said "what kind of a coincidence is that"? i handed her the book and said "its yours, i'll go find another". she smiled and walked to the check out line. i ended up with a book of short stories of science fiction. the very first chapter told of two strangers who met in a library and how he gave the book to her, only to meet her again at a later date. this was too weird and the following week i went back to return the book. there she was again sitting at a table and reading something i just returned. we looked at each other with amazement and finally spoke our first words. after that there was a silent kiss which happened to be the last chapter of her romance novel and my science fiction book. so where does coincidence, reality, and fantasy begin or end? we didn't try to figure it out, we just went along with it. one year later we got married, the same day our library cards expired....*

last call...

the lights flashed indicating it was last call as the bartender set up the drinks. "this one is on me" he said. a few sips and then one last trip to the men's room. it was the sound of an engine that wouldn't start in the parking lot behind the bar. she left her lights on and the battery was dead. i tapped on her window and offered her a ride home. a thank you and a wide smile said goodbye to me as i left her front porch. a phone number was found in my shirt pocket the next morning. two weeks later we met at the same place and got to know each other. the bartender smiled at the both of us and winked. he must have known something that bartenders often do. a few months later we sat on the same stools as i handed her a ring. she said yes. the lights flashed at our wedding and we never left when there was a last call...

window dressing...

the lighting was just perfect and the props were set in place. both mannequins had been dressed in their winter attire as michael then stood outside the display window for his final approval. he was the manager and lead designer of the display department in a well known shopping mall. his social life left something to be desired but the lonely 30 year old found comfort and love within the confines of a window that sold merchandise. winter turned to spring and then summer as michael was promoted to store manager and vice president of operations. he still had his hands on involvement in dressing the windows and with nobody else around he would talk to his favorite lady mannequin. june rolled around and michael hadn't shown up to work for a few days and neither had he called in sick. the personnel director just got no answers when she tried to phone his home. one of the crew stepped outside his display window to make a final check on wedding outfits for a june bride sale. he had to look two and three and four times at the groom as what he saw was just kept to himself in disbelief. michael stood motionless next to a secret favorite lady mannequin where a first time smile could be seen under the perfect lighting....

the seashell...

the seashell whispered the waves to me long after i had left the beach. it was a reminder of summers gone by when you were with me. those teen years of a first love that lasted a few seasons was a treasure in my heart never to be forgotten. it was a small seashell that hung around my neck for over twenty years since then. i found myself on that same beach once again re-living the moments we had together. some twenty feet away a lady sat on a blanket as she stared out at the oceans waves. she held something up to her ear which was attached from around her neck. i listened to mine and heard a whisper of my name beyond the sound of the waves. footprints walked towards each other as she also heard her name being called. a full moon smiled down from above as it once did before when it recognized two young souls of a first love once again remembered. we kissed for a second time and it was recorded and played back on a beach of our desires....

16 candles...

16 candles adorned her birthday cake on this very special occasion. the rented hall held about 200 guests which consisted of her friends, classmates, relatives, etc. she seemed to stare often at the drummer of the live band that was hired for the event. they spoke during a break and exchanged phone numbers. the napkin which she wrote it on was lost somewhere on the way home as so was his. the last thing they remembered was a slow dance that was played by piped in music while the band was on a break. time passed until 20 years later she attended a dance club which played oldies music. i looked at a girl in the corner of the room and stopped playing as my drumsticks dropped to the ground. the bass player announced a sudden short unexpected break and she stared back at me. piped in music played "unchained melody", a slow song we had danced to 20 years before. there was a second kiss as we exchanged napkins this time that was never to be lost again. the rented hall for our marriage ceremony had 16 candles...

indian waterfalls...

indian waterfalls was a name given by my camp counselor at a resort in the catskill mountains. every summer my parents drove us there while growing up from a 5 year old until I was 23. now at 50 years old I had to go back for a reason which was not yet known. the same path was there that led up a mountain climb that lasted about two hours. there it was right in front me, indian waterfalls. another twenty minute climb would lead to the top of the mountain overlooking the countryside below. I heard the stampede of horses though there were none to be seen. a smell of smoke and the burning of tents filled my senses as women and children fled into the valley below. my sneakers became a pair of moccasins and my walking cane became a bow and arrow. it was a place where I had lived and died before that needed a spirit to go back home. a gentle breeze blew the fresh green grass just in front of a tent where my princess greeted me. and so the soul comes to rest again where love never dies, just postponed. we climbed down about 20 minutes and sat together holding hands just above indian waterfalls...

the autograph...

it was time to clean out the attic and either save or throw away the items there. sara peeled off the old rotted tape that held shut the huge cardboard box. there was some thirty years of stuff packed away as she laughed at some of them wondering why were they saved. other items had sentimental value and she stored them in a new box that would be taken to a new home where she was about to move. in her new home sara unpacked and set up the house as just she wanted it to be. at the bottom was a book which she didn't really look at in great detail while sifting from the attic in her old place. the white cover still had its brilliance and the title never faded at all. on the inside cover was a signed autograph from its author to a fifteen *year old girl which shook some precious memories back to the surface of the now 45 year old. it was a labor day weekend back in 2008 where it all happened. she remembered looking at him with loving eyes and how they hugged together in a moment of inspiration and caring. michael looked in his attic and tore off some old rotted tape from a huge cardboard box. he was about to move to a new house and needed to sort through some thirty years of items to be thrown out or saved. he kept a book that was written by him and a photo copy of a short story about sara. the condo had two floors and one morning he walked down the steps as she was just about to leave the front door. sara turned around and their eyes and memories met once again. the hug was more intense this time around as an angel signs an autograph to events subscribed to those readers who believe...*

imaginary date...

since we never met in person, let me take you on an imaginary date. sit back and enjoy the evening as it unfolds...its a comfortable 68 degrees in early october as the time and date came to be. we met on a specific corner in manhattan and the place in question was a five block walk away. you complimented me on my jacket and tie as i returned it with one on your dress of choice. it may have been our first date, yet we automatically held hands, a sign of a good beginning. the elevator took us to the 65th floor of the restaurant that overlooked the city below. a window seat was ours made by a reservation two weeks earlier. it was on a slowly moving revolving platform that this place sat as the streets below would change views. drinks and dinner were served and we danced shortly afterwards to the live band on a platform in back of the room. our last dance was a slow one when the lights dimmed and we whispered in each others ears. i slipped the waiter a few bucks and he took out the rose that sat in a vase on the center of our table while you were in the ladies room. clear cellophane was now wrapped around it and i asked you put your hand under the table for a surprise. "thank you michael, what a romantic gesture", you said with a warm smile. i beeped the chauffer on his cell phone as he waited on the street below. he dropped me off first and then took you home. you set the rose in a vase on your kitchen table and then went to sleep. it turned out that we spent xmas and new years together as family and friends both approved our imaginary date. the following october a wedding took place on the 65th floor of a building where we first became acquainted. the band played our favorite slow dance as you smiled when underneath a table i surprised you with a rose wrapped in cellophane...

fair lawn home ...

fair lawn home was a place for the elderly. apple sauce and oatmeal that were easily swallowed became a main stay diet along with a blue pill that helped them sleep. a black and white TV hung in the lounge where old and new shows were broadcast to those who remembered. the game room had checkers and chess along with various card games where winners and losers would say goodnight without remembering the night before. me and susan sat together for the first time over a game of checkers. i was 96 at the time and she was 91. her finger had a ring on it that looked so very familiar. the blue stone reminded me of high school some seventy years ago. i looked at her and asked "do you remember where that ring came from"? "yes michael, i do", she said. we didn't take that blue pill on this evening as neither one of us wanted to go to sleep. we snuck past the exit sign and walked outside without anyone noticing. the two of us couldn't be found the next morning but it didn't really matter. beyond the exit somewhere in a place where we eventually go stood two people. the school bell rang at the end of june as i placed a blue ring on her finger...

a porcelain angel...

just above my computer desk lay a porcelain angel. her eyes were closed and she slept there with a permanent smile on her face. her left hand rested just beneath her chin as one wing covered her from the waist down. i gave the name angelina to this figure and each night before i signed off, a kiss would be placed on her forehead. she was a *comfort to me and a silent companion as i lived alone. the ankle bracelet was cut down and fitted with a chain link and clasp which i put around her. our initials m&a had been engraved. to what lengths a lonely soul would go through is just a personal experience which the outside world need not know about. i thought there was a tear in her eye when i signed off the next evening, but maybe that was just my imagination. with a full time job i decided it was time to hire a part time maid to help with some cleaning around the house. after a few interviews i picked who i thought would be best for the job. she had her own room as a sleep in guest and performed her duties well and beyond what was expected. the bedroom window was left open as an unexpected cold wind blew through the house. her blanket was partially off of her feet and when i attempted to adjust it, there was an ankle chain which caught my eye. the initials m&a shocked me into a reality which i never expected. i ran back to the living room and the porcelain angel was no longer there. her eyes were closed and she slept there with a permanent smile on her face. i wiped a tear from her eye and my angelina kissed my forehead...*

venus 2 diner...

i reflected on some old good times and memories of the mid 70's. the carefree weekends back in brooklyn where dance clubs, bar hopping, and a ride from a car service that took me back home again. my intention was to find a girlfriend and maybe establish a relationship, but it never came to pass. too many one night stands were all these girls seemed to be looking for. i guess it was payback time for all the hurting and lost loves that they once were looking for. the last stop before the car service was a place called the "venus 2 diner". my meals were always the same. manhattan clam chowder soup, a lettuce salad with french dressing, a cheeseburger and fries, and for dessert two cups of coffee. that was the highlight of those weekends back then along with a safe ride home. in 1995 some twenty years later i drove back there to give it a second chance. the names of the clubs and bars had changed and the dancing wasn't the same anymore. it was still a young crowd and i felt out of place. the venus 2 diner was still there which again was to be my last stop. a waitress approached my booth as i caught a glimpse of her name tag. it looked so familiar but i just couldn't remember why. she said, "how about some manhattan clam chowder, a lettuce salad with french dressing, a cheeseburger and fries, and two cups of coffee for dessert"? a sudden flashback of me and Carol had us on a ride home from a car service with a one night stand that should have lasted longer. "i got nothing to go home to tonight, how about you"?, she said with some tears in her eyes. we rode back home and made love for the second time. she introduced me to a daughter that was conceived by us some twenty years before. i asked her to marry me in front of our daughter and all agreed. it wasn't the typical meal you would have at a wedding, but me and the wife thought it appropriate for this special occasion. manhattan clam chowder soup, a lettuce salad with french dressing, cheeseburgers and fries, and 250 cups of coffee...

the doll house...

it stood about three feet high and four feet wide with two levels and fifteen rooms. the object in question is dorothy's doll house, a place where a lonely child had her true friends. mom and dad left her alone too often with baby sitters and the attention she needed was focused on the little figures that stood inside. dorothy played with them as the chef would cook her meals, the maid would clean her rooms, and the gardener would cut the grass. she made the chaueffer doll drive her around to do some shopping in a mall that existed just beyond the property. the chef fixed her a birthday cake as mom and dad were always too busy or not at home. on her eleventh year dorothy was nowhere to be seen by the baby sitter. a panic stricken sitter called the parents as they rushed home and searched the house. the police came and a missing child report was filed. nobody thought to check the doll house as a little black limo and a chauffer were gone. somewhere outside the property dorothy went shopping at a mall where she made new friends. now adopted by caring and loving parents she blew out real candles from a real birthday cake in a world where we often escape too. me and dorothy share a new house together as husband and wife. you see, i was the chauffer who took her away....

the cellophane rose...

on the way to school i picked a red rose from a garden in the park. i wrapped it in some cellophane that i took from my parents kitchen drawer. the love of my young life went to the girls room and i placed it on her desk in front of me. she picked it up upon returning as the bell rang to let us out of school. her kiss on my 8 year old cheek was where it all began. in high school fate had us together again after we had forgotten some previous years. the man in the flower shop wrapped a rose in cellophane and this time i attached a card. i placed it on the desk in front of me as she went to the girls room. just before the bell rang, she read the card and kissed my 17 year old lips. in college fate had us together again after we had forgotten some previous years. at a wedding of a mutual friend i was the best man and she was the brides maid. we talked of years gone by as i walked her home that night. a block before her house was a park with a garden. i picked a rose and wrapped some cellophane around it which i saved from my heart. a best man and a brides maid soon had their own wedding which was remembered from previous years...

a snow flake in July...

it began to snow lightly down upon an ice skating rink in the middle of manhattan. i picked up a wool hat that the wind blew off from the girl in front of me. she turned around and fell on the ice when i tripped over her as we both had a good laugh together. "you lost your hat and then we both lost our balance", i said with a smile. she tucked her hair back under the wool cap and we continued skating together. there was a bar we decided to go into on that level of the rink in order to warm up a bit and continue our conversation. the night ended with a goodbye kiss and the exchange of phone numbers. a snowflake fell on my nose and that was a sign of a future event that never would have been expected. it was in july of the following year that we have now been dating for seven months. she told me what happened when she left the rink back in december with the same story of a snowflake falling on her nose also. maybe a sign of a bigger event to come. on a park bench we sat together and i reached into my pocket. she opened the little black box and stared at the engagement ring which i then put on her finger. for some unknown reason we looked up at the summer evening sky as two snow flakes landed on our noses. it was a special event that no weather man would have predicted, but for us it was a sign of love confirmed...

something meant to be...

after high school graduation the summer had me and my girlfriend on a beach one july summer evening. in my pocket was a box that contained a gold ring with a blue stone and the inscription of midwood high school, 1965. in my other pocket was a 14 karat gold chain. i slipped the ring onto the chain and held it behind my back as she walked from the waves to the sand under the boardwalk. "turn around and face the other way, i have a surprise for you", i said. my fingers clasped the chain shut around her neck and she turned around with a special look of love in her eyes. we danced under the boardwalk that evening and on a blanket made love for the first time. in 1985 i reflected back on that special occasion and drove back to where i used to live. the waves and sand and boardwalk was still there. a seagull squawked a familiar sound as a lady walked slowly from the waves to sands just in front of and under the boardwalk. something swung from her neck back and forth and stopped just below her neck. a gold ring with a blue stone stared me in the face. "michael? is it really you"? she said with some tears in her eyes. on a saved blanket that i held from special memories we made love for a second time. i don't know why i had an engagement ring in my pocket that night, but i guess it was something meant to be....

angels and screen names....

michael felt that there wasn't much time left as he lay in the hospital bed. the tubes and wires reminded him of a complicated radio he once tried to build and put together from scratch. his life was reviewed in the lonely part of his brain that wished for something special before his time was up. that chance came when the nurse handed him his daily notepad as he scribbled neatly something that surfaced from a very long time ago. it was a combination of some letters with a few numbers which formed a screen name that he once knew. the nurse saw a tear in his eye and felt that this was something he really needed. she smiled and promised him to write to this e-mail address with his request. the lady in question opened her mail and wondered how after all these years he had remembered her. "you have a visitor", the nurse said a few days later. she looked at him with a question of sadness in her eyes, yet happiness at the same time for being able to meet him. michael scribbled on his note pad "i wouldn't let the angels come for me until i had seen you." she squeezed his hand and kissed him on the cheek. Michael's vital signs rose from nearly flat to a steady healthy rhythm. he pulled the wires and tubes like an old radio he once tried to build and sat up with a twinkle in his eye. he spoke for the first time and said to a lost part of his life "i love you". let the records show that the spirit was healed as so was the body in a hospital room where very few miracles are reported. my name is julie and i was the nurse who discharged him from the hospital with a clean bill of health. a month later i got an invitation to their wedding....

it didn't really matter...

from memories of a childhood that spanned twenty three years, let me take you there on this journey through time....it was during the summer months that mom and dad drove to the catskill mountains to a hotel that was owned by my uncle manny. the sound of the pebbles and gravel in the parking lot crunching under the tires of our car had me know that we arrived. to the right of the main house was a small playground with a few swings and a see-saw. those were my earliest memories. the main house consisted of two floors and outside was a casino where entertainment was provided with movies, bingo games, comedians, etc. there was an outdoor pool up on a hill and a baseball field about 50 yards away. eventually through the years new bungalows were added along with more rooms for new guests. about a hundred yards past the baseball field were the campgrounds where us kids would roast marshmallows and hot dogs under the supervision of a camp counselor. down the road was an entrance to the woods which led to indian waterfalls where we would catch salamanders in a shallow stream. the opposite walk had us at a small store with comic books, snacks, food, drinks, and a pinball machine. my guess is that these years spanned 1950 through the mid 1960's. my uncle had long since died and the name of the place had changed along with a new owner. now 40 years old i pulled my car into the parking lot as the pebbles and gravel still made a crunching sound beneath my tires. i ran around the bases where i use to play ball and then walked forward to an old campfire site with some stones that still remained. it was december and the hotel was closed but for me it was just another summer, just another memory. "remember when we shared some marshmallows and hot dogs"? a voice said from behind me. the snow fell but neither one of us cared. i'm not sure whether i was still 40 or 15, but at that point it didn't really matter...

209 pages later...

the back cover of his book had her intrigued. there was a nice photo of the author with a short description of himself and what the book was about. she ordered it from an online site that was found through some research of books that may have been of interest. it was soft cover and 209 pages long as she picked it up from her mail box just outside her front door. each short story was about two or three pages which made for easy reading and to continue at another time. it was in the quiet and solitude of a public library that she read the last few stories. her heart and soul was touched by the depth and meaning of what the author had written. the last line on the last page read "in the quiet solitude of a public place, there we shall meet". he sat there next to her and she instinctively turned to look at him. "it is you that have met me here, just like the last line of your short story". it was 209 days later, just like the length of his book that the two of them got married...

as my dad tucked me in...

a buddy of mine, litegrneye@aol.com has recently lost her father. therefore this mail is dedicated to her, but shared with all others who have dealt with the same grief.... i sat on his knee when just a child and he read me a favorite story until it was time to be tucked into bed. sometimes he would let me sleep between him and mom when i had a nightmare and was afraid to be alone. dad always knew what to get me for x-mas without a clue of me telling him. sometimes mom wasn't around so he helped me with my homework and also put a band-aid on my scraped knee when i fell. he was my counselor, my mentor, my guardian. i fixed him some hot chicken noodle soup when he got sick often during the winter months and sometimes during the summer i would apply ice cubes on his forehead when running a fever. dad would drive me around to where i needed to go before i got my license and picked me up when it was time to go back home. he often put flowers in a vase and set it on my night stand just to say how much he loved me. there were times when he told me "i won't be around forever, so please listen to your mom and do the right thing." i knew he was sick yet his passing was never expected as dads are so supposed to last forever. an empty vase was suddenly filled with flowers on my night table and then i knew he was still around. he whispered an old favorite story of mine in my ear just before going to sleep. my blanket was pulled over me with unseen hands as my dad tucked me in...

those little things in life...

i counted maybe six or seven young ladies waiting on a line to get into their rest room. the crowded bar apparently didn't have enough stalls and i let the ladies enter the men's room after i checked that it was all clear. i appreciated the thank yous and even got a few kisses on the cheek. it was those little things in life that made a big difference. on the way to work a homeless man sat on a park bench just staring into space. i walked back to the street vendor and bought 2 more hot bagels with cream cheese along with a large cup of coffee. he looked at the paper bag that i placed next to him and opened it up. his weary tired eyes twinkled and smiled at me as that was all i needed without any words needed to be spoken. i picked up a wallet in the elevator and then got off my floor at work. on my lunch break i found 300 dollars in cash, six credit cards, and a photo drivers license of an employee in my same building. i traced it and went to her home and returned all the contents intact.

she offered me a big cash reward but i turned it down. it was those little things in life that made a big difference. the rewards for helping others are just the simple satisfaction of knowing the right thing was done. strange as it may seem, some ten years later a bartender served me a drink and showed me an old faded white paper bag that he saved from a bench so many years ago. "this one is on me my dear friend" he said. i cried and hugged him across the top of the counter and we talked of how his life has changed. it was those little things in life that made a big difference. i waited on a line to get in the men's room and this lady opened the door on her side and watched as she let me in. "you let me in ten years ago, remember? i kissed you on the cheek and then you found my wallet and returned it to me", she said. my best man at the wedding was a bartender who served home made bagels with cream cheese. my new bride found a lost wallet of mine in the men's room and laughed at the picture on my drivers license. it was those little things in life that made a big difference...

a red phone makes a call...

the clock struck 11 am as a young man was approached by the uniformed guard. "any last requests"? he said "how about bacon and eggs done over easy and a cigarette afterwards"? a tray was slipped beneath the cell as Joey ate his last meal. the twenty five year old was then led to a chair with straps and head gear that would run some 50, 000 volts into his body. the scene is death row and a priest walks behind the condemned man saying the usual prayers. the guard pulls out a half lit cigarette from the young man's lips who takes his last puff. he is asked if he wants a blindfold but the young man shakes his head no. a doctor stands by behind the glass with a stethoscope to make sure the prisoner will be pronounced dead. "any last words"? the priest asks. "may God bless my innocent soul, for i have not committed the crime that i was charged with". the executioner stood with his hand on the switch at a moment before 11:30 am. the red phone rang as a uniformed guard waved off the final pull of the switch. "stop the execution" the governor screamed into the phone. joey was unstrapped and a new trial was set by the governor who found new evidence of the real killer. dad sat before the court and admitted to framing his son in the murder of his wife. the governor was convicted as his son was set free from all charges. his admission of guilt led the jury to a minimum sentence of 25 years to life with the possibility of parole. 15 years of good behavior had dad released from prison as his son joey met him outside the prison gates. they drove home together as an angel held a red phone with guilt and innocence in the balance. justice goes beyond the court system when the truth and a guilty conscience comes to light. chalk it up to a judge above us where a red phone makes a call...

the next tree...

there was a tree in a state that we both have been to before. it was in our childhood that our initials were carved into the bark with a pocket knife that left an impression never to be forgotten in each of our memories. a place i had to go back to and re-live the month that we were together. two teenagers in love for the first time left that mark to be found once again. i was drawn to the same exact location and stared at our initials for the second time. you tapped me on the shoulder from behind and asked "is this the place where we first met"? a month went by where two adults were kids again and made love for a second time around. he took out a pocket knife and walked to the next tree as she held his hand. ....

rubber bands and paper clips...

one story above street level i looked out my bedroom window. it faced the back yard with a tree in the garden below. spring was here this particular april and i took out my rubber band with a box of paper clips. i would shoot them at the leaves of the tree, just a fun thing to do at the age of twelve. a bird cried out and flapped its little wings as it fell from the branch of the tree. it was an accident with no harm intended and rushed down stairs to street level and ran out the back door. a baby bird lay there with one wing flapping. i picked her up and brought the little creature inside the house with tears in my eyes. a home made splint was made as i carefully attached it to the broken wing. she was nursed back to health and i climbed the ladder of my tree house and placed the precious baby back in her nest. mom flew back with some worms and fed her daughter once again. i threw away my rubber band and box of paper clips so this accident would never happen again. my prayers were answered and i thanked God for saving her life. my time was up some years later from my hospital bed where I heard the flapping of wings. a mother bird greeted me with the wings of an angel and took me away. i chirped from a branch on street level in a backyard where there are no more rubber bands and paper clips...

violin lessons...

violin lessons began for debra at the age of seven. it was a request to her parents where this talented yet young soul displayed her hidden gift of music. she excelled in the high school and college band and at the age of 22 was discovered by a talent scout who eventually booked her at a solo performance in madison square garden. a standing ovation applauded this young genius who touched the hearts of each who listened to her perform. later in her life she played her violin in some of the most memorable movies which won academy awards. at the age of 40 her body succumbed to a fatal bout with pneumonia. i sat next to my daughter's bedside in those final moments and cried a lifetime of tears. there were thousands who lit candles at a vigil who attended the loss of this most talented soul. her violin sits in my bedroom beneath a window where the stars shine outside. a wand crosses it strings and keeps me up at night where dreams and reality blend together. debra continues to play and kisses me on the cheek goodnight as she plays the love of violin lessons continued...

her first ride...

she was seven pounds and eight ounces, twenty two inches long. behind the glass a nurse held her up from the other side of the window as i waved at my new daughter. mom died during child birth so i had to raise her and be both parents at the same time. when she was ten years old the school bus let her out as usual on the block that i lived on. my usual walk across the street to pick her up was interrupted by a speeding car that took her young life away. under the xmas tree sat a pink bicycle, a ride for my ten year old that never made eleven. the snow fell outside and continued through new years day which i really didn't want to be a part of anymore. there was an angel ornament on top of the tree as she watched me point a pistol to my head. my finger froze and a voice whispered in my ear..."this is not what God intended for you. do you wish to go back"? my tears pleaded yes and then i stood outside a room with a glass window. she *was seven pounds and eight ounces, twenty two inches long. the nurse put my daughter back in her mothers arms and i smiled at the other side. her mother unwrapped a pink bicycle under a tree for her tenth birthday. we both held her steady as she went for her first ride...*

our beloved pets...

what we get from our pets is unconditional love. some have four feet and others have none. some swim in a tank and others have wings. the sounds of their communication to us is endless and each one has a special pair of eyes that connects to our heart and soul. there may be a wild deer crossing a country road and since it is a creature of God, she or he is also my pet. they need not be in our possession or in our homes, just in our hearts. i have now bella and stella, two cats which are mother and daughter. from childhood memories there was randy the parakeet, jack the dog, cindy the canary, harvey the hamster, stuart the snake, jill the gerbil, tara my rabbit (one that didn't rhyme with the first letter). last but last least was felicia the firefly. those who have past on come back in dreams, those who are still with me do that also. our pets love us as we do them and guess what? they heal and comfort us when we need it the most. her orange body with four black dots on her back recently entered my room. she smiled at me from Gods eyes and introduced herself as laura the ladybug....

december 24th, 2,012, eleven p.m. ...

december 24th, 2,012, eleven p.m. ...my dad was a gentle and loving soul. his depression and loneliness often was reflected in his book of "incredible short stories". he never showed it though as i was growing up and the times he cried was always hidden from me. he put on my first band aid and healed every wound after that. mom died during childbirth and my father was also my mother. matters of the heart he often preached as opposed to textbook studies i struggled with in school. "your lessons come from living, not from reading", he often said. his password was saved on the log in screen and i learned a lot about his buddies and the chats and the e-mails that were sent and received. he seemed to have something of an obsession about meeting others in person. maybe that was part of his loneliness. i read the 209 pages of his book which described his heart and soul in every detail. maybe where he is now, the writings continue and my dad finally met someone in person. if nobody else is there, then i shall surely be when my time is up. i miss you dad and love you very much. i hope my band aids heal your wounds. love, scott...

mei ling...

her jet black hair and blue eyes didn't seem to be a typical trait of this oriental waitress. i would wonder about this as a strange attraction would *have me come back to the restaurant many times. she wore a name tag which read mei ling and flashbacks fluttered through my mind but they stopped with explosions and a helicopter taking me away. a picture of her sat on the wall just behind the checkout counter with a lady who i guessed was her mother. there was a ring on the mothers finger which was out of focus, but none the less, still there. in my dreams the flashbacks became real once again from a war i used rage through. there was a high school ring that i thought was lost but it was on her finger there in my dream. i went back to the restaurant and the waitress handed me the check and i noticed a detail that may have been missed before. it was a ring that i gave her mother before the daughter was born. some things are passed down and this had my memory become clear and focused of an event during the vietnam war in the year of 1967. the waitress agreed for me to meet her mother as i told her we knew each other before. mother and daughter shared the same name and the daughter had my blue eyes. she held the ring up over her head and spoke to all of the familiar customers in a language i partially understood. the crowded restaurant stood on their feet and cried as me and mom and our daughter hugged and kissed. no more flashbacks except for the time we cut the wedding cake. the inside of the wedding band had us connected, me and mei ling...*

the summer of 1965...

two teenage girls clutched the see through iron fence while watching some teenage boys play basketball. "that one in the blue shorts is really cute", one said to the other as they both giggled. the girls walked around the opening of the court and sat on one of the benches to watch us play. i commented to one of my teammates "that girl on the bench over there with the white shorts is really cute". the game was over and we all went our separate ways, including the two on the bench. next weekend i went to my friends birthday party at his parents house just about a block away from where i lived. guests came in at scattered times throughout the evening and at about 9pm a familiar face was seen on the couch just across a few chairs from where i sat. her party dress was very pretty as a flashback had her on a bench last week watching me play basketball. "hey, i remember you" we both said at the same time. she took a napkin and wiped off some ice cream cake that sat on my cheek. from then on the night passed by too quickly as it usually does when you are having a good time. i put a clean fresh napkin in my shirt pocket where she had written her phone number. we talked the next week when i called her and my parents phone bill probably jumped up over the course of the next few months. we dated for almost two years and eventually we got separated by different colleges and two separate states. that was the summer of 1965. these events were fresh in my memory *some twenty years later and i longed to go back to where it all began. i parked my car on the same street where a basketball court still stood. i held the original ball which i had saved and walked through the opening by myself on a late saturday evening. the park lights shone down on the quiet cement and i stood under the basket, ready to take a shot. ten fingers clutched the iron see through fence and watched me. her footsteps were quiet and silent until she sat on a wooden bench where her white shorts caught my eye. in my shirt pocket was a napkin which i took out and wiped away the tears on a cheek as was done before to me. we got married and for some reason that was only special to us, the album cover read, "the summer of 1965"...*

the swimming pool...

mom fell asleep on the lounge chair with a drink in her hand. it was by the shallow end of the pool where she was supposed to watch her 7 year old daughter. i sat on my lifeguard stand by the deep end and watched the little girl walk over to my side of the pool. she started to run and suddenly slipped and fell into the ten feet of water below. it looked like she hit her head on the side of the pool just before she fell in and i jumped off my platform and dove in after her. the sound of an ambulance siren woke the mother up as i explained what had just happened. the pool was temporarily closed and i drove the mother to the hospital. there was mild head trauma but the doctors said within a week she should she be just fine. we picked her daughter up in a few days and the little girl put her arms around my neck and kissed my cheek with a thank you. mom looked at me and did the same. i introduced my also 7 year old daughter and as both being single parents we seemed to have much in common. i quit being a lifeguard that summer and took a pay cut as a waiter who would serve breakfast only so that me and mom and our daughters could spend more time together. the little girls became close as if each needed a sister to be with. me and mom became close as if we needed a partner to be with also. the following summer i didn't work there anymore, but just a guest this time. a band set up by the deep end of the swimming pool as two little 8 year old bridesmaids held the long flowing white gown behind my wife to be. she tossed the flowers behind her and wouldn't you know it, they landed in the swimming pool as we all had a good laugh...

the playground...

a half hour recess had the public school kids in the playground just across the street. down the sliding pond they slid as others would climb the monkey bars or bob up and down on a see-saw. i can remember her name was gail and that her pony tail swung back and forth as she rode the see-saw. we often held hands on the school bus that drove us home each day. that was where we kissed way in the back of the bus where young lips first met. i often wondered why this memory of thirty years ago would stick in my mind, but never had an answer. maybe if i go back there i'll find out why. on a saturday afternoon when school was closed, i walked across the street from my old public school and watched the fall leaves blow around the playground. my long adult legs stretched across the pavement as i sat on a see-saw that used to have some meaning. quiet footsteps entered the playground as the lady behind me said "mind if i sit down"? we bobbed up and down for a while as her pony tail swung in the breeze above her head. "hi, my name is gail, remember me"?

it was bella...

my tenth birthday fell the same time as it did every year, christmas eve. i was the only child and so that made each present even more special than the one before. it was a strange looking box under the tree which had a handle on top and holes on each side. mom and dad said "go open your present". the two week old kitten was sitting there curled up in a ball fast asleep. she shook her head and woke up as she meowed her first greeting to me. i hugged mom and dad when i cried a tear felt thank you. fresh food and water every day along with cleaning her litter box was my responsibility which i took on with great care. i named my new furry friend bella. the seven inches of her little body fit perfectly in my hands when i picked her up to give a kiss. bella would purr herself to sleep and lay a paw on my face on the same pillow we slept on. we would play together with my toys and she was my best friend. i folded up some aluminum foil into a ball and she would chase it and bring it back to me. that became her favorite toy for months and years to come. time passed and i reached twenty two years old. Bella was now about twelve and she seemed to slow down a bit. on her fourteenth birthday her rear legs would drag across the floor as she stopped to lay down and rest. her breathing became slow and soon she stopped eating and drinking. i held her close and said "go towards the light my precious girl, God is waiting to take you home". one last meow, one last look from her fading blue eyes. then a paw on my face to hug me goodbye. i ran into my parent room that christmas eve and just stared at them with tears running down my cheeks. i am now alone at my own apartment at thirty two years old. it was christmas eve that i went into the kitchen and opened a drawer. i folded some aluminum foil into a ball and let it sit under the tree. it rolled into my bedroom while i slept and then a meow was heard as a paw hugged my face on a pillow it was bella...

it was just a card...

it was just a card sent in e-mail wishing her a happy birthday. she smiled and remembered him with a thought that somebody else cared. the mail man *delivered a singing telegram wishing her a merry christmas with a single red rose from the sender. it was placed under the tree as an unexpected present. the months went by as each occasion was remembered by him. valentine balloons floated in her house and rested on a pillow where she dreamed of him. her phone was quiet with too many "leave a message after the beep" played in his concerned ear. it was a long drive to where she lived and he found out from a neighbor of hers that she was in the hospital from a car accident that left her in a coma. he spoke to her softly while kneeling at her bedside and proposed his love to her. in a dream she was handed a black box and she opened it to find an engagement ring which was in fact set on the bed before her. one teary eye opened and the other. she whispered yes with lips longing to meet his. maybe it was a few cards or something more that had them meet for the first time. a single red rose and a few valentine balloons floated over the bride and groom where i took the pictures and documented this story of "it was just a card"..*

the last entry...

while cleaning out some drawers from the various rooms in his house, he found an old address book. it dated back some twenty years when bar hopping and exchanging phone numbers was the thing to do. there were friendships written along with one night stands and possible relationships that could have been. a thought crossed his mind to dial again, but logic took over and he knew these people would have either moved, got a new number, or just plain not remember. the last entry had her full name and the bar address of where they met. something inside his gut told him to go back there and he drove the fifty miles on what happened to be the exact date and time of when it happened twenty years before. while cleaning out some drawers from the various rooms in her house, she found an old address book. the last entry had his full name and the bar address of where they met. she drove some fifty miles on what happened to be the exact date and time of when it happened twenty years before. his mind called out her name with a question mark as she did the same on a bar stool sitting next to him. it was answered when both showed each other the last entry...

the healing...

it all started from a rented room upstairs where i used to live. there were six including mine where us tenants would share one bathroom and a kitchen. no set schedule for what needed to be done, each of us had to play it by ear. me and karen were friends and she worked the late shift in a hospital from 10pm to 7am. she would get home about 8am and knock on my door with two cups of coffee and a few donuts. we spent about a half hour together chatting until i had to go to work and she had to go to sleep. it was during one summer morning when the event took place that changed both our lives. she put down her cup of coffee on the kitchen table and then uncontrollably began to cry. "i'm tired of this body, i'm tired of this life", she moaned. karen rolled up the bottom of her pants leg uniform and then her arm sleeves. needle tracks ran up and down her leg and arm. what happened next i can't explain why i did what i did or why i said what i said, but this exactly what happened..."hold my hands and close your eyes, do not speak until i ask you to", i said to her. thoughts of suicide entered my brain as i picked up every emotion she ever felt. my hands started to sweat and my heart raced as i felt my my inner being shaking to its core. i took on the pain and suffering and then somehow shook it off as my breath became stable once again. "open your eyes and tell me what you feel", i said. "i feel like dancing, singing, i feel happy and don't know why, but i just love it", she replied. the needle tracks had disappeared from both arm and leg when we looked again. karen is now clean and sober and currently is the head nurse on a daytime shift. she has since been married and has two children by a doctor at the same hospital. how or why this healing took place i have no idea, yet i know that it has happened. a second time some twenty or so years later occurred over the computer with a friend from texas. a woman who was born deaf who was my friend's neighbor had her hearing restored by at least 70%. i believe it will be fully *restored when eventually we meet in person as my friend and her neighbor should move to new york where i am now living. if you think i am making this up, then you can contact carol from texas and she will confirm her neighbor's ability to hear once again. her address is <u>txcritterlady@aol.com</u>.*

teddy and blanket...

teddy and blanket covered and slept with him in his first five years of life. the warmth of the small yellow blanket and the big brown eyes of the stuffed animal was all he needed to fall asleep with. i kept those two items stored in a curio cabinet in my living room to remind me of my son. he never reached his seventh year of life and my dreams of playing ball with him and doing all the things that a dad usually does with his son, never came to pass. mom died shortly after and the house that once had a family was no longer there. just a few photos of us along with teddy and blanket. in a dream i asked God to take me away and He said unto me "your time shall not be accepted now, so go and awake to a new beginning". there was a small yellow blanket that covered me when i awoke and big brown eyes smiled from a teddy bear next to the pillow on which my head rested. i played ball with him this time around and mom cheered him on when our son won the championship little league baseball title. i became a grandfather and in my son's living room was a curio cabinet that displayed teddy and blanket...

the good humor man...

it was somewhere back during the 1950s that i recall a childhood memory that i believe we have all shared. for me it was june, july, and august that the white truck drove down our street at 3pm ringing its bells. it was the good humor man with a picture of a chocolate bar on the side of his truck. mom or dad would give me a dollar bill as i read the menu posted on the back. the prices ranged from 10 cents all the way up to 50 cents depending on what you wanted. next to the price was a small picture of the item so you knew what it looked like. popsicle, icicles, fudgesicles, ice cream in a cup with all different flavors and toppings. sprinkles with or without syrup. the line was always long but well worth the wait. most of us knew ahead of time what we wanted. i can even remember that his name was jack which stuck to his white shirt on a black nametag. sometimes mom and dad would let me keep the change from the dollar bill for the next time the good humor man would return. what amazed me most was how he opened that silver door on the back of the truck, stuck his hand in, and pulled out what you wanted without him even looking inside. there was always this little girl behind me and i let her in front of me on the line. her pony tail always swung around and hit me in the face when she thanked me for letting her go first. the old neighborhood was still there as i parked across the street from where i used to live. it was 3pm as a white truck drove down the street. i lost track of time but didn't really care as i pulled out a 5 dollar bill. there was a lady behind me who politely asked if she could go ahead of me on the line. her pony tail swung around and hit me in the face as she thanked me. maybe kids and adults grow up again together in a time and place that doesn't really matter except for what we need to go through again. we got married at 3pm and if you listen carefully, there may be bells heard from a white truck coming down your block. listen for the good humor man...

one large pie...

on those cold winter months every friday was a ritual when i ordered one large pie for me and the girlfriend. sometimes with extra cheese, sometimes with pepperoni. we would snuggle up together on the couch and watch a good movie as the slices slowly disappeared. her name was diane and we met in our senior year of high school. our romance lasted through three years of college until her dad had a job promotion which had the entire family move out of state. that was back in 1975 and i remember kissing her goodbye at the airport just before she boarded the plane. there went my first true love, never to be seen or heard from again. twenty years past and during the winter months of 1995 i sat alone as the doorbell rang. it was late december just after christmas and right before new years. a delivery boy stood there with one large pie in his hand. "i didn't order *any pizza here, sorry you must have the wrong house", i said. he confirmed my address on the receipt but i was still puzzled. "may i use your phone sir to confirm who placed the order"?, he asked. the boy hung up and turned to me and said, "it was called in by diane". a horn honked from outside from my front door and went to look and saw a hand outside an opened drivers side window holding a cell phone. the large pie had extra cheese and pepperoni as a long lost lover and i sat on the couch again as we watched a good movie. the wedding was plain and simple as my bride and i made some slices return and then disappear from one large pie.*

a starry june night sky...

it is on a still lake that we sit under a starry june night sky. the paddles lay silently just beneath the surface of the water where the time for rowing had ceased. guilt for not having been able to save her a year ago had me stare into the lake with thoughts of joining her. frogs started to croak as if they disapproved of my intentions. a cabin that wasn't there a year ago had a light turned on where through the window pane a figure stood opening two small curtains. a hand waved at me and i felt the need to find out why. the frogs grew silent and just sat on their lily pads and watched me knock on the front door. "why were you sitting out there by yourself"?, my girlfriend asked. she was there right in front of me, alive as if last year never happened. i held her close and begged for her never to leave me again. to this day i can never explain what happened for sure and i gave up trying to analyze it. all i know is that a cabin still remains where we live now under a starry june night sky...

a november wind...

this is love story which may have happened or will happen. no states or names will be mentioned to protect the identity of those involved. she parked her car out in the street just outside of the condo complex he lived in. it was a semi circle with a garden in the middle and if she walked to the left of the garden and straight ahead, there would be his address. they were 2 years apart in age and have met online in a site where members share each others thoughts and ideas and writings. emails and conversations of a past life had too many things in common for it to be a coincidence. he met her outside and knew that she would be there at a time when his instinct said so. a real hug took place instead of the usual brackets surrounding a screen name on the computer. they held hands while both entered his dwelling. there was something in her state that couldn't be found which was sicilian pizza. he ordered a large pie and she tasted it for the first time. a three day and night visit had them catch up on things needed to be said and done. a november wind blew outside but the warmth within remained the same. her hand rested beneath a pillow next to his as an object was felt. she woke up and a held a small black box that was there. the engagement ring fit perfectly on her finger as she shook her partner awake and said "i do". the june bride looked lovely inside a church where outdoors whispered a november wind...

always there...

i am the grasshopper which jumps from each blade of grass in your front lawn. i am the butterfly who lands on your window sill looking in. you pass me by in the street and turn your head around for a brief moment. remember a dream from last night? who left you flowers without a card from who it came? a door bell rings while you sleep and a phone leaves a message that you may have erased. i still cover you with your own blanket as you sleep and dream. never to be alone as i am always there...

FOREVER IN BLUE JEANS...

they stood on opposite ends of the platform as both trains approached, one uptown and one downtown. why they looked at each other through the trains window was something yet to be understood. it was a friday morning when each walked up the steps to cross over to the other platform in the hope of meeting each other. "i don't know what to say, i just know that i had to meet you", he said to *her. "exactly my intentions", she replied. they both agreed to call in sick that morning and spend the day together. the two of them boarded an uptown train and walked to the midtown museum. he was dressed in a suit and tie, a successful manager from a well known real estate firm. she wore blue jeans and worked downtown in the garment district living pay check to paycheck. there was a five year difference of age as he was the older and she the younger. her english wasn't that good but he understood the young spanish girls' meaning. from the museum they went to eat out at a fast food joint and took in a movie in the early evening that friday. a date was set for saturday night as they both went their separate ways back home. he wore blue jeans and when he picked her up and because there was no talk of what to wear, she answered the door in a beautiful dress. they both laughed out loud as she said, "let me get into something more comfortable." six months later there was an outdoor wedding performed on a beach where both of his and her guests dressed as they wanted or not wanted to. there was beer and champagne, spanish rice and prime ribs of beef. tortillas and hot dogs, and every other american - spanish food you could think of. the one thing the bride and groom had in common was that it was informal for them as they both wore blue jeans. it was a unique wedding where two different cultures and two different life styles blended together in such harmony. i was the wedding photographer and can attest to this fact. the cover of their wedding album had them kissing beneath a full moon on a beach with the waves set in the background. at the request of the bride and groom, i had to label the front cover "FOREVER IN BLUE JEANS".*

a familiar song...

there were new rides and old rides that remained in a amusement park called coney island. nathan's famous hot dogs and fries were still there and the pink cotton candy still swirled around the stick that it was made on. the same clowns face stood above the tunnel of love ride and the cyclone still had youngsters screaming as it raced down the steep tracks. below the wooden boardwalk waves crashed on the sands and the same song of the seagulls could be heard. it was the merry go round that triggered a flashback as a teen back in 1958. the sound of a little girl crying because there was no more room on the ride. i remembered the back of my horse had room for another as i waved to her parents and they stopped the ride so she could get on. the thirteen year old put her arms around my fifteen year old waist. she said "thank you". i remember her waving goodbye as she left with mom and dad. she turned around and blew a kiss that stuck with me for twenty years. at thirty five i felt a little uncomfortable getting on a merry go round for kids, but it was something i had to do. a 33 year old rode on the back and she put her arms around my waist. we walked under the boardwalk

and kissed as the waves crashed against the sands,
and the seagulls sang a familiar song....

plain and simple...

and so the physical attraction continues. she looks
for a stud, a handsome dude, nice car, money, etc.
he looks for slender body with a beautiful face,
nice hair and eyes, etc. then each of them opens
their mouths to speak without thinking of the
dumb things they say. neither one listens, they just
follow each other for a temporary commitment
that lasts not much longer than a one night stand.
my blue-green eyes stays focused on the one with
a heart and depth of character. outer beauty is a
shell that often loves its own self in a mirror. for
me the plain and simple outshine them all with
something special that dwells within the heart and
soul. they have the quality to give and not take,
to share and to understand. behind her glasses
lay blue-green eyes just like mine who think the
same. we never asked of each others age or how
much money the other was making. our first date
wasn't in a fancy restaurant but at a take-out in
front of a fast food window. the wedding was in
my backyard behind a basement apartment that
i lived in. only twenty five guests, but who cares?
it was plain and simple....

yellow creek bridge...

yellow creek bridge separated two towns in tennessee. its two hundred foot span was where she snuck over to my side on some weekends and I did the same to meet her. my parents were rich and owned a mansion as my girlfriend was a poor farm girl who knew nothing but the simple life. both our parents objected to us seeing each other and we were caught many times together on both sides of yellow creek bridge. there was a feud between their town and ours which I never understood even though daddy tried to explain it me. his political references had my 14 year old mind not in tune with his. all I wanted was to be with my 12 year old Nellie. the quiet Friday night was shattered by the sound of gunshots on a night where it was my turn meet her on that side of yellow creek bridge. she waved her hands for me to go back as she fell to one knee. I ran the whole two hundred feet towards her as bullets flew across the bridge from both sides. we dove into still water below and swam until we reached land, not knowing which side of the bridge we were on. I tied her red bandana around the leg she was bleeding from. her farmhouse and my parents mansion were eventually burnt to the ground as a civil war between towns finally ended. in the summer of 1967 some twenty years later, a young man and woman walked slowly towards each other and met in the middle of a bridge. they didn't have to look back this time as she handed him a red bandana to heal some old wounds. I put a ring on Nellie's finger as one town celebrated our marriage from both sides of yellow creek bridge...

as i rode back home...

dad ordered a bicycle from a catalogue and put it together a few weeks before my birthday. the year was 1958 and i was eleven years old. the july sun burst through my bedroom window on a saturday morning which was my birthday. "wake up sleepy head, there is a present for you waiting on the front stoop" dad said. while still in my pajamas i raced to the front door and peeked outside. my first bicycle stood there waiting for me. dad had already laid out my clothes as i got dressed and ran outside. the red hornet stood there and dad picked me up and sat me on its seat. red streamers flowed on each of the handlebars and a horn button was attached to the right side of its body. two mirrors and a hood mounted flashlight on the front fender had me in awe of this gift from dad. i rode around the block at least 500 times as dad approved of my new riding skills. i carved my initials on the rear fender m. r. my bike was stolen one week later as dad filled out a police report but it was never found. in 1998 i attended an antique show of old motorcycles and bicycles. there was a red hornet behind the ropes on display which looked so very familiar. the red streamers, the two mirrors, a hood mounted flashlight. i asked *the guard if i could look at the bike more closely and he let me under the rope while watching me with curious eyes. my initials m. r. were still there on the rear fender. i showed a valid identification of michael reisman and explained my story to him. the manager let me take my bicycle back to its original owner. my feet were a little longer now but i still pedal the same way as i did before. maybe some angels or spirit guides had me go there to find something stolen from my childhood. i beeped the horn and turned on the flashlight that night as i rode back home...*

the flashback...

it was a familiar scene that flashed back to my mind when i saw the ten year old too far out in the deep water of the pool. a leg cramp had her sink and her little hands splashed above the surface as i dove off my lifeguard platform. i held her and swam to the ledge when i lifted her out and then gave mouth to mouth. she coughed as i rolled her over and then pushed hard on her back as she spit up the remaining pool water that once filled her small lungs. mom woke up from a lounge chair where she fell asleep and rushed over to her daughter. they hugged in relief that life was spared. mom and daughter thanked me as for the rest of their summer vacation we all spent together. i told her of an event that happened twenty years ago where my own daughter was in the same situation but i couldn't save her back then. our friendship turned into something more during the next few months as the single mom and me decided to get married. i found it strange that her daughter had the same first name as mine who passed away exactly at the same age. her daughter who is now 20 and ours as far as i was concerned pointed something out to me. it was a birthmark just below her right shoulder. it was a familiar scene that flashed back in my mind when my daughter was first born. "daddy...is that you"? she said with tears in her eyes....

it was rachel's call...

rachel was about to attend the super bowl where her favorite team was going to play. she followed her team from 6 years old up until now at the age of 14. the cancer in her body wasn't going to stop her from missing this event. rachel knew every call and formation as if she had the playbook right in front of her. the fourth quarter came with two minutes left on the clock as we were behind by 3 points. it was fourth down on the opponents 30 yard line and a field goal would send it into overtime. the coach sent out the field goal unit and rachel screamed out no no go for it! her favorite quarterback was the holder for the long snapper as he stepped back waiting for the kick. in her mind she called out "fake field goal, roll right, screen pass to the tight end" the quarterback turned is head up to the stands where she sat for a brief moment before the ball was snapped. he *waved his hands as the audible was called and the play was changed. he rolled right as the tight end snuck down the field and caught a perfect pass as he rambled into the end zone for a touchdown. her team had just won the biggest game of their lives and rachel became the loudest fan cheering. the "make a wish foundation" for terminally ill patients allowed her to attend the game plus visit the locker room for a post game press conference. the quarterback looked at the 14 year old and said "she was in the stands and whispered to me the call that won our game" the team, the press, the coach all gathered around her as she spoke. "i'm just 14 and dying, but now i can go knowing that my team won the biggest game of their lives". the coach gave the game ball to rachel as most important player. she is now in heaven and i am sure my daughter has found a team to coach among the angels who have her now with many game balls to come....*

parents unknown...

the birth certificate read as follows...last name first name, then saint johns hospital, new brunswick canada. born 6 AM, parents unknown. i had nothing to go on and no leads to trace my family history, so I guess July 29th, 1947 was all where it started and ended. there was nothing wrong with being adopted and i accepted that as a fact of life and treated my parents as the real mom and dad who raised me. It's funny how now my favorite beer is molson golden, imported from canada. i was now living in the united states and had no memories of canada since my adopted parents brought me here at the age of 3 months old. i forgot about trying to trace my roots a long time ago and just went on about my life at the present age of 35. my first true girlfriend showed up at a high school class reunion and we hit it off quite well together. marriage and a son and two daughters followed some years later as time flew by and suddenly the wife and i reached our 65th birthday. we rummaged through a trunk in the attic which contained some old items, photos, documents, etc. from our younger years. she found her old birth certificate and then said to me "know what?, i never could trace my family history since i was adopted". "same here", i said. we compared the certificates and they both read saint johns hospital, new brunswick canada. July 29 1947. she was born at 615 am shortly after me. parents unknown.....

the last seven minutes...

just before closing there was a slow song. we spent the last seven minutes as strangers no more. i can still see your face and hear your words even though the years came and went without us ever meeting again. the bar was still there just down the road about a hundred yards from the motel on a highway to nowhere. it was a place we traveled before, forgot about, and then suddenly remembered. the bartender now had some wrinkles and gray hair but his voice was the same. "hey man, i remember you" he said with a smile. we talked of old times if only for one night remembered. "where's the girl you danced with that night"?, he asked. i just shook my head and said "i wish i knew". maybe it was a calendar that was marked on a certain date and time for a second chance. just before closing there was a slow song, we spent the last seven minutes as strangers no more....

a fluttering of wings...

i heard the fluttering of wings just before i went to sleep but no birds were in sight. a tooth lay under my pillow as mom and dad told me the tooth fairy would replace it. six year old Michael fell asleep and the following morning there were two quarters under his pillow. "mom, dad, look what i found. she came and left me these". at seven i heard the same wings and just assumed it was my favorite tooth fairy. Michael found a dollar bill the next morning and put it in his private piggy bank. she was an imaginary friend i often spoke to in my dreams. her name was adele and we played often while i slept and also awake. before i knew it, there were no more teeth to leave under a pillow but i kept her in my mind and heart anyway. now at thirty years old, Michael answered his front door for an interview with a prospective house keeper. I heard the fluttering of wings just before i opened the door. "hello, my name is adele"...

serena...

dad surprised me with my first ever pet. it was my twelfth birthday and he unwrapped the small carrying cage of which he took out a small kitten. brown in color with bright blue eyes and a little pink nose. "thank you dad, i just love her so much" i said. "take good care of her, she will be your new friend for life", he replied. i held her in my arms and she touched my face with her little white paws. fresh food and water was a daily habit i maintained as i gave her the name of serena. she curled up on my pillow each night and her tail touched my face which i thought was her way of holding hands. the nine inches of her young life bloomed to twelve, then fourteen, then twenty as she became an adult in the cat world. each meow had a different pitch and length which i came to understand of what my serena was trying to tell me. she never really outgrew her childhood playfulness as i watched her chase around the paper and aluminum balls i made for her. her tail no longer rested on my face, it was now her front two white paws which hugged me goodnight. when i became twenty four and she became twelve years old, serena slowed down a bit and didn't drink or eat like she used to. her meows became weaker and i felt that something was wrong. dad told me that the age of cats may vary and their life span is very unpredictable. i watched her tummy breath less and less as she lay on my pillow and i cried for her not to leave me. I knew then it was time to speak my final words. "go towards the light my sweetheart, God is waiting for you". her blue eyes closed and her white paws touched my face to say goodbye. those were the memories i had of my beloved first pet serena....

in a wire framed garbage can...

she rubbed her hands together in front of the fire that was lit from old newspapers in the wire framed garbage can. then she curled up beneath a torn blanket when the winter winds finally blew out the flames. i was coming from work that night when the usual walk through the back alley wasn't the same. i tapped her on the shoulder and held out my fresh hot cup of coffee and she sipped on it with a small smile. the scarf around my neck i took off wrapped it gently around hers. "come with me and warm up for i shall not let you suffer here anymore." the fifteen year old told me a story that would make the most hardened criminal cry. "take a shower and here are some new clothes for you that my sister left behind. hot soup and then a plate of macaroni and cheese awaited her she as gobbled down both as her smile widened and her eyes became clearer. the young girl slept soundly in my bed as i slept on the living room couch. she stood over me the next morning with two cups of coffee and hot pancakes on the kitchen table. we talked some more and that day she agreed to live with me. on her twenty first birthday she accepted my engagement ring and we made love *for the first time. just before our wedding trip to the chapel, we both looked out of my window which overlooked the back alley below. some old newspapers lit by themselves in a wire framed garbage can....*

the friendship club...

once a month the friendship club met at a dance from this grammar school function. the boys and girls would usually sit and stay in opposite corners of the room. it happened to be a slow dance before the night was over and i put down my cup of fruit punch at the table where i was sitting. she did the same from across the room and we met half way with the same intentions in mind. a few words were spoken as a first hug and kiss left a lasting impression for years to come. it was strange that thirty years later we both lived in the same neighborhood once again. a new bar opened up and the name rang a bell from many years ago. it was called "the friendship club". before the night was over a slow song played. i put down my beer at the table i was sitting at and she did the same. we met half way with the same intentions in mind. more words were spoken and we caught up on lost years gone by. our second kiss and hug lasted a lot longer this time around. strange how in front of the church we got married was a sign post stuck in the green grass. "the friendship club"....

between 7 and 7 and a half...

in his mind he saw a ring size between 7 and 7 and a half. she responded in the instant message "wow how did you know that?" "i'm sort of a sensitive and psychic, so i just had to put that out to you" he replied. they were to meet in the month of november for the first time as she would drive from michigan to new york. it was eleven am in the morning when she parked her car that saturday morning. he stood in the street and waved to her when the drivers side door opened and she got out with a huge smile. it seemed to be in slow motion when a hug and a kiss evolved just on the sidewalk a few feet away. they walked together hand in hand towards his apartment and chatted live and in person without the usual keyboard. her stay at a nearby motel was canceled as the three days and nights were spent with him at both their requests. he slipped a ring on her finger while she slept through the night. it was between 7 and 7 and a half that made a perfect fit. she noticed it when she awoke as he stood beside her bed with a question waiting for an answer. her eyes and smile told him yes. it was about one year later at their wedding when the clock struck 7:15 p.m. somewhere between 7 and 7 and a half...

a red scarf...

chestnuts on an open grill along with hot dogs and burgers filled the air on street level just above the skating rink below. there was also hot baked salted pretzels that the street vendor would sell with a spread of mustard as an option. there was no wind and the temperature was a chilly but comfortable 38 degrees. i put on my ice skates and circled the rink with the rest of the crowd in a circular motion that had us all go with the piped in music from above. a lady in front of me slipped and fell down so i picked her up as she thanked me. it happened three times and then we finally talked. it was her first time skating and my fifth so we just continued while holding hands. our tired feet gave way to having a drink in the bar-restaurant on the same level as the rink. it felt good to have our regular walking shoes on again. the place was heated and so we removed our jackets, gloves, and scarves as the bartender sat our drinks down on the counter before us. time flew as usual when there is a good time involved and we both had to go home. the casual meeting came to an end as we both said goodbye. she left her red scarf on the bar stool and i took it home with me as something to be remembered. the same vendor was there next xmas and he pointed down to the rink below showing me someone who i had missed for about a year. he gave me two hot dogs and said "this ones on me, now go and surprise her again." i caught up with her as we circled around the rink and said "feel a little bit hungry"? we sat on a bench and ate our hotdog's as we talked of old times from last year. "hey, that's my missing red scarf around your neck", she said. i took it off and *put it where it originally belonged. neither one of us fell down anymore and the bartender said "this ones on me". next december there was no wind and the temperature was a chilly but comfortable 38 degrees. about two hundred guests stood on street level and below on the rink. we said our vows as a ring was placed on her finger, and then a red scarf...*

want to dance?

its a bird or a cricket. maybe a frog on a lily pad that sings its song. no headphones involved or a radio station, just natural music. i can hear your fluttering of wings as you hear my buzzing about a busy hive. we have a slow dance together in a world of the big and the small. you see, we are not much different from each other. my wing knocks on your door as a paw opens it. want to dance?

see through fence...

across the street and a little to the left was a sand lot surrounded by a brick wall and wired fences. it served as a place to play soft ball with the various boys on the block where we used to live. it was the memory of that place from 1953 that took me back there. i still cry over the sad and tragic event that no 14 year old should ever have gone through. my 1973 ford was parked just across the street and my 34 year old eyes remembered it like it was yesterday. it played out again in my mind like watching the reel of an old black and white movie. a classmate who was also my first girlfriend stood behind the fence on the sidewalk looking in. "come on mickey, lets hit a home run" she said. the softball hit the top edge of my bat and spun backwards over the fence. "i'll get the ball" she yelled as she ran backwards across the street without looking. i saw the car racing down the street heading towards her and screamed for her to get out of the way. it was like watching an event in slow motion when she turned to look at me as the car slammed its brakes. she flew over the hood and then rested on the pavement behind. i watched the ambulance take her away as the softball spun around with traces of red on it. my 34 year old fingers clutched the fence and i cried again as i did so many nights before. my 1973 ford suddenly disappeared and i heard some old buddies of mine say "hey Mickey, want to play some softball"? i stepped up to the plate and awaited the first pitch. my girlfriend shouted from behind the fence, "come on Mickey, lets hit a home run". i didn't swing the bat this time nor did i for the next two pitches as i struck out. no foul balls over the fence, no girlfriend chasing it. the speeding car ran down our street once again, yet no brakes needed to be used. we grew up together this time around and drove our 1973 ford to a second honeymoon....

the babysitter...

sharon the babysitter tucked in the seven year girl at about nine o'clock that saturday night. she had about two hours to kill as the parents should be home by eleven. she sat back on the couch and turned on the tv and flipped through the channels. the doorbell rang at ten thirty and sharon awoke from a short nap thinking the parents got home early. "may i use your phone please? my car broke down and i really need to call a tow truck, the stranger said. "i'm sorry, she said. i can't let anyone in here right now" as she started to close the front door. his large foot stopped it from closing and then he pushed it open. her screams were muffled when he put his hands around her throat as she blacked out. the seven year old woke up and walked down the stairs as she peeked over the banister to see the stranger carry Sharon into the basement. the little girl dialed 911 and spoke in a whisper as she told the dispatcher what had just happened. "don't leave your room and lock the door, we are sending help right now". the parents arrived at the same time the police did as they had to wait outside of the house. the babysitter regained consciousness and watched the intruder walk back up the basement steps to the main floor. she raced up and grabbed his ankles and then pulled as hard as she could. he tumbled backwards and fell back down the stairs as his neck broke. a six month long investigation and search of the serial babysitter killer murders had finally ended.

sharon was never charged with the murder of this beast who stalked a town in fear for half a year. she was instead awarded with a substantial amount of money and a gold badge of courage from the governor of this state and the mayor of that town. mom and dad especially thanked her for keeping their daughter safe. i reported this story in a place where it all happens too frequently and may i say that sharon is now my new babysitter...

for the second time...

there are places we go back to visit with special childhood memories. for me it was an amusement park in brooklyn , n. y. the place was coney island. waves crashed under the boardwalk just stopping at our toes as we laid on a blanket there. it was where we first kissed. i can remember handing you a teddy bear that i won at the shooting range with pistols that burst colored balloons. we shared pink cotton candy and rode on just about every ride that was there. the parking lot was full as usual and i could smell those famous hot dogs and fries and corn on the cob. some rides were updated and the people there were different from before, but the heart and soul of this place still remained. there were some painted horses that rotated on the carousel which especially attracted my attention. that was the ride where we first met some forty years ago. i handed the man my ticket and he looked at me rather strangely like what is this 60 year old doing here on a ride for kids.

a 57 year old lady gave him her ticket who was just behind me on the line and suddenly the ticket taker understood what was about to happen. he un strapped the buckles of two teenagers and smiled as me and you shared some pink cotton candy as we held hands while walking under the boardwalk. the waves just stopped at our toes and we kissed for the second time..

her curly blonde hair...

her curly blonde hair swayed in the wind as the see saw bobbed up and down in a playground where we grew up. her name was norma jean she was my girlfriend in those early years. we signed each others year book at graduation and continued to date on through high school. at seventeen she became a pin up girl and was posted on quite a few calendars. after graduation she was noticed by hollywood and we lost contact after our first real kiss of hello and goodbye. fame and fortune followed her as i was left behind with just a few memories of a playground and signed graduation books. marilyn was her stage name but i always thought of her and still do as norma jean. maybe after she passed away and went to heaven, will she look back and smile at me for the time we never had together. my time came and i went to heaven also as i asked God "is she still here? where can i find her"? he sat me on a see saw and on the other end was my first love with curly blonde hair. we grew up together without a pin up girl on some calendars and not a trace of hollywood was to be found. graduation year books were signed and eventually a marriage license. it was an outdoor wedding and her curly blonde hair swayed in the wind....

1981, 6am...

it was after some chats that i asked her about her profile picture. she told me it was from 1981 which blew me away. i replied that mine was also from 1981. this goes beyond coincidence for sure. a background of Indian blood in our veins from a family tree had us in more of a strange connection which we felt from the beginning of meeting here online. the similarity of tastes in food, music, lifestyle, and many other things had us wondering what is this all about? the subject of birthdays came up in one conversation and she asked "what time were you born"? 6 am i replied. "me too", was the response as we both sat silent for a minute before talking again. we agreed to meet in the month of november in person for the first time. i just stood on the sidewalk while her car pulled up and parked against the curb. it was a dream of seven and a half that had me go to a jewelry store just a week before. i slipped it on her finger which happened to be the right size where coincidence was tossed out the window. she said to me "gray wolf, is that you"? "yes my little fawn", it is i. the last thing i could remember was that it was now 1981. the wedding seemed to be a little earlier than most would have had. we said "i do" and a rooster crowed just outside a church at 6 a.m. ...

it was a summer park...

she was born deaf but her eyes took in what needed to be seen and not heard. a few miles away he was born blind but his ears took in what needed to heard and not seen. it was the summer in a park that they both often went where they met for the first time. she sat on the bench next to him and petted the seeing eye dog that laid by his feet. he could hear the wagging of his companions tail and knew that there was a friendly presence next to him. she spoke the best way she could and he replied with a gentle squeeze of her hand. it wasn't easy, but somehow the two of them found their own way of communication between them. in the months to come they moved in with each other and on that first night something very special happened. she heard him whisper in her ear as they made love for the first time. he saw her smiling eyes as the sun rose the following morning through a window that was opened by an angel they never saw or heard. the dog no longer led him around but still stayed as his companion. she heard the wedding bells ring and he clearly looked at her when the priest said, "you may now kiss the bride". it was a summer park that they both still go to now where you can see and hear them, including the wagging of a dogs tail...

welcome to mike's barbeque...

its that time of year again where we are ready for our first barbeque. let me take you now to my place for a virtual experience at mike's cook out...the backyard is over 1,000 square feet long and holds comfortably about 50 or so guests, one of them being you. it is now memorial day weekend as you arrive at my house. a full moon lights the grass below and the temperature is a nice 72 degrees. four grills are already lit with steaks, burgers, hot dogs, chicken wings, and corn on the cob. bottles of mustard and ketchup with paper plates line the tables scattered about my yard. an electronic bug repellent sits silently in all four corners of the property to insure a pest free environment. large bowls of light green iceberg lettuce with ten different dressings is available for salad lovers. a separate table with baked ziti, lasagna, and Chinese food sits in set up hot plates in the center of the backyard. four surround sound speakers sit in each corner playing pre-recorded tapes of music from the 50's, 60's, and 70's. there are two bathrooms in my home, main floor and one flight up for those who need to go. soda, wine, beer, mixed drinks are available with four large tubs of ice at each table. there are 3 guest rooms in my house and also a motel one block away where i have reserved 20 rooms for those who wish not to travel back home and rather spend the night. at two o'clock that morning all the guests had already left. i did my clean up and put everything *away as i was now ready to retire to bed for a well deserved sleep. "i didn't feel like going home tonight or checking into some strange motel. do you think I can stay here with you"?, she said. we both had a drink in our hands and somehow it was the last call and toast of the weekend. the morning sun glistened through my bedroom window. it smiled its rays of sunshine on a face next to me where a pillow used to be empty. you held my hand and the following summer wrote out invitations for the next barbeque....*

a vacancy sign...

the motel sign had the vacancy flashed in its red neon sign. it was just a point in the road of his journey to a quick stop for a two day rest until his final destination. the bar just down the road had nightly entertainment and he sat down at a quiet table and ordered a beer. the waitress returned and asked if there was anything else he needed. he showed her an old photo of his missing daughter from twenty years ago and asked "ever seen this girl before"? her memory flashed back to a time when she ran away from home and then said, "yes, that's me". "forgive me daddy, but it was something I had to do". he put his arm around her shoulder and they walked together outside of the bar and went back to the motel as they both checked out. his car made a U-turn and went back to new york where it all began. she hugged the mom that she hadn't seen her for so many years and the three of them caught up on times that were missed. somewhere on a highway from a place to go to and a place that needed to be returned to was a vacancy sign that was fulfilled...

the gift...

the gift was delivered by hand with no special occasion. it was a rose picked from a garden on the way to school and left on her desk as class was dismissed. 12 year old samantha turned back around as a scent of a flower filled her senses. it was from a shy boy who sat behind her just showing that he cared and was interested. it happened again in high school and then in college as she wondered who was this mystery man? her doorbell rang one new years eve some twenty years later as a shy young man stood there with a dozen roses now bought from a flower shop. "may i come in please, we have to talk", he said. she invited him in as it was 10 minutes left until the ball came down for the new year. his face looked familiar but the shyness seemed to disappear as he spilled out feelings from so many years gone by. memories and dreams ended up with the click of two glasses when a gift in person finally presented itself...

laura...

laura was a 17 year old cancer patient who hadn't much time to live according to the doctors. it was two years before this sad news that she was smiling and happy, just your average high school freshman student. she was an aspiring writer who just read about half way through a book she ordered online. some of the stories touched her heart in a special way and she felt a need to meet the author in person. laura finished the book in her hospital room and asked the nurse if she could reach the author. i received an e mail and a lump in my throat and a pain in my heart hit me with something i needed to do. it was a short flight from my city to hers and then i got a cab driver to take me to the hospital she was in. laura recognized me from my photo on the back cover and smiled through the tubes that were attached to her mouth. she held my hand as i signed the book she most treasured in her heart. i handed her my second book "where angels tread" and signed that also. "keep reading my sweet laura and keep your faith and belief in what you hold dear to you", i said. she hugged me with weakened arms as i left the hospital. a phone call to me one week later was from the head doctor who was in charge of her case. "laura would like you to pick her up from here as she has fully recovered and no traces of cancer can be found. i don't know what you did, but in all my years as a doctor i have never seen a terminal patient completely recover like this before". it was a short flight from my city to hers as i waited outside. laura got in my car and said "i finished your second book"....

roommates...

she answered an ad i put in the newspaper for a roommate to share expenses in my two bedroom apartment. the 800 a month rent would be split in half which would make our budget for living a whole lot easier. we both had our privacy with each of us in our own bedroom as we would share the kitchen and food and utilities. after six months of living together with guests coming and going, we both decided that it was not what we needed or wanted. our outside search for companionship was actually there within from where we lived. our baby had a room to stay in as the second bedroom became our daughters room. we got married the following year and i saved the ad from a newspaper that changed our lives. 20 years later our daughter lived on her own in an apartment with two bedrooms. he answered an ad she put in the newspaper for a roommate to share expenses with utilities included. i walked her down the isle as dads often do when the wife and I gave away our daughter. she had a son who put an ad in the newspaper some twenty years later...

where time is of the essence...

two people met online as he was 61 and she was 59. there seemed to be a special bond between them from things in common and it eventually led to a romantic interest. they laughed and giggled as *the years from their physical body was taken over by a mental state of how they felt. "i feel like 21 again", and she replied "i feel like 18". after about a year they finally set up a meeting between the two of them. she drove to his house and opened her car door and stepped onto the curb where he was waiting for her. behind his back was a single red rose and he thrust it out in front of her with the shy look of a teenager love struck for the first time. they kissed and hugged while a late model car of hers turned into a 1958 chevy. her pony tail swayed in a november wind as his black leather jacket was zippered up to the top. they went to a drive in movie and watched rebel without a cause starring james dean. and so two old folks had become young at heart where time is of the essence..*

goldie...

on my tenth birthday dad surprised me with the first pet i ever owned. she came in a small tank of water and was about two inches long. a beautiful goldfish with green plants that swayed in the water just above the small sand pebbles below. i named her goldie. she followed my finger as it traced the movement along the side of the tank. her eyes never blinked and dad told me that was the way fish were. little fins fluttered back and forth just before she blew little bubbles to the surface. by my twelfth birthday dad told me that we needed a bigger tank since she was growing and needed more space to swim around in. i fed my goldie every day and cleaned the tank twice a week as recommended in the manual. there was something more however as special bond and love between us and nature took place. i would kiss the glass and she would respond by doing the same from her side. on my fifteenth birthday i woke up to feed her. goldie was just floating on the top of the tank and her fins weren't moving anymore. maybe if i sprinkled more food she would wake up, but she didn't. dad held me tight and hugged me as my tears fell on his shoulder. i scotched taped two wooden toothpicks together and stuck them in the dirt in my backyard garden where goldie was laid to rest. when i was twenty five years old, i met some one and fell in love. her eyes never seemed to blink but i never thought about it at the time. she always wore yellow clothes and then told me of her nickname goldie....

a candle, a slow song...

the citywide blackout occurred when there was a full moon above. it was the only source of light outdoors and somehow the heavens knew it. those who were lucky enough had radios with live batteries to listen to the news of what had just happened. on our small street block most of the neighbors sat on their porches with flashlights and lit candles as they walked amongst each other for conversations on this scary event. people who knew each other by sight or maybe just a wave of hello or goodbye suddenly became close friends. for the next six hours we all wondered when the power would be restored. batteries finally went dead for those with updates on the news as we were just left with candles, a few flashlights, and words of how we shall survive. some of us shared cold slices of pizza and others just looked up above at the moon, the only spotlight on a darkened and chilly october evening. a neighbor who i had never seen before started crying as her candle dripped the last melted wax over her snuffed out light. she came into my home and with the last two batteries I placed them in a portable cassette player. we shared some leftover potatoes and then i pushed the play button. it was a slow song as the candle flickered just beneath a full moon above. suddenly the lights went on and the power was restored. two neighbors saw each other in a new light and kept on seeing each other until he put a ring on her finger. at the wedding there was a candle, a slow song....

zelda...

it was an uncommon name that I gave her, zelda. beneath the hair and eyes and clothes was just a steel frame with circuits and memory cards. zelda was a companion - house maid which performed her daily chores around the house while I was at work. the year was 2,025 when most of us had this kind of help around the house. some nights we would play a game of cards or checkers or chess. other nights we would just watch television together. zelda would cook and clean and make the most spectacular dinners you could think of. I would often come into her room while she slept and just stare at her for awhile, wishing she was human. in a way she almost was. her sensors detected smoke and heat coming from my room one night this cold December evening. she lifted me out of bed while I was totally unconscious and carried me outside the house. she blew breath back into me from her metal lungs and I awoke to find her laying down and very still. one eye opened with a tear in it as her lips smiled and spoke for the last time, "you are safe now, but my system is overloaded with emotions I do not understand. shutting down now". there was a special place where robots were laid to rest and I visited her with some roses in my hand. an ad in the paper had a real live human come to my house for an interview. I hired her and she told me her name was zelda. one eye opened with a tear in it as her lips smiled...."prologue or afterthought" - maybe steel frames with exteriors of what looks like us is something more than that. maybe there is soul somewhere between the circuits and the memory cards. you are invited to attend the wedding next December of michael and zelda...

little fawn, gray wolf...

there was a mention of some american indian heritage in their chats as two friends became a lot closer than expected. a bond was established from things in common and possibly the loneliness in their lives. he called her little fawn and she called him gray wolf, two names made up from maybe a past memory that we yet have to understand. they finally met in person and dated for the next couple of months. a vacation was planned in the mountains of Pennsylvania. they hiked up the mountain through the forest and trees and came to rest at a boulder rock just on top of the mountain. there was a lone tree just behind them bearing fruit as they both picked the berries from the branches. the bark revealed some initials carved some hundreds of years ago. L. F. loves G. W. one horse rode away with 2 souls sitting on its back to a time where they now live again....

in the arms of a stranger...

i got an e-mail from a concerned mom about her 17 year old daughter. it read something like this..."dear michael, my daughter doesn't know you but she read your book and wishes to meet you in person. she lays in the hospital dying of a blood disorder and keeps calling out your name. she would like an autograph and to see who has touched her in such a positive way. can you please come to my state and visit her"? without a second thought I booked a flight and drove to moms house and we hugged each other. then we both entered the hospital and took the elevator to the fifth floor. I kneeled beside her bed and took out a pen to sign her first autographed copy of this precious girls book. she flipped the pages and stopped on page 17. it was a short story of an angel called angelina, a nurse who gave hope to a dying young girl who eventually took her back home to heaven. mom cried behind me as i held her daughter in my arms. i stared at the screen and watched it go flat line as the doctors rushed into the room. "not on my watch", i whispered into the little girls ears. the staff was puzzled and amazed how she recovered fully and left the hospital with a clean bill of health. a single mom raising a daughter had now a second chance to be together again. i entered their lives and we became a family. in the arms of a stranger...

a frog, a prince, a knight in shining armor...

a frog, a prince, a knight in shining armor. such are the dreams of the young and old alike. patricia had her share of frogs before growing up and wished no more of that. it was time to meet a prince or knight in shining armor. her 59 year old body held the mind and soul of an 18 year old whose dreams are always kept alive. she agreed to meet a 61 year old man whose ideas were basically the same, maybe a princess. on a cold november morning she parked her car on a street just outside from the complex of apartments that he lived in. he stood there on the sidewalk with a fresh red rose wrapped in cellophane in his hand.

it was the first time he gave one and the first time she received one. a warm kiss wiped away the cold november wind as they held hands and walked to his apartment. it was under a xmas tree that they sat together in the month of december. there were no gifts exchanged, just the unwrapping of each others love. on top of the tree was an angel which was already there from past experiences in their lives. they had a daughter together through a marriage which happened some months later. she kissed a few frogs and then met a prince who was her knight in shining armor. he handed her a red rose as she parked her car on a street just outside from the complex of apartments that he lived in...

a prom dress...

30 percent comes from my mind and 70 percent comes from my heart. it is a balance of figures from which i write stories that may be fiction or truth. this is one of those stories...mom helped her daughter get into her prom dress for the big upcoming event of a high school graduation. there was a party afterwards at a rented local restaurant where all would meet and celebrate. a designated driver would take her home, a boyfriend of the four years they spent together. a red light at a railroad crossing had them stop but the car skidded onto the tracks from the heavy rains that wet the streets. it stalled as a loud horn blasted its warning. he got out of the car and raced to the passenger side but the door was stuck shut. it was a memory that haunted him for the rest of his life. michael got an invitation to a high school reunion at the age of 45 years old. he stood there in the same restaurant and looked for a girl who he once loved. the prom dress looked familiar but it was just a misty apparition of what once was. "take me home" was a whisper in his ear as they drove to a red light at a railroad crossing. he grabbed his girlfriend and immediately left the car before the sound of a loud horn blasted its warning. maybe some angels adjusted time and circumstances where 30 percent of their mind and 70 percent of their heart came into this story. my wife and I often look into a closet where we saved a prom dress...

the painter...

tonight there was no live model to paint a portrait of, so he sat in front of the canvas and used his imagination. the brush dabbed on the pallet and mixed the colors as he started to paint. her lips were thin but had a fullness about them as a slight curl on either side made them smile. the chin was rounded yet small and petite. her nose was plain and simple yet distinctive just below her blue-green eyes. the brows were thin and was almost covered with the bangs of her brown hair just below her forehead. tomorrow he would add the finishing touches to his canvas. one final stroke had a pendant necklace with a gold heart attached. his *fictitious lady he randomly gave a name to. it was stephanie. a well known art gallery bought his painting and in a few weeks it was displayed at a famous museum in new york. he beamed with joy at the recognition of his unknown portrait hanging on the wall of this well known museum. the rich and famous often went there to bid with prices not affordable to most of us. he sat down and watched the crowd bid on his painting. the young lady next to him outbid everybody else to the sum of one million dollars. he noticed familiar features like a fullness in the lips, a slight curl of a smile, a petite but rounded chin, and a distinctive nose just below her blue-green eyes. she took off the pendant necklace with a gold heart attached and handed it to him with a familiar smile. "hello, my name is stephanie"....*

from many pages to come...

the owner of the liquor store flipped the store sign around from "open" to "closed". it was 10pm on a new years eve and he cleared out the days receipts from his register. a tap on the front window had him turn around and walk to the front door. a young lady stood outside with a pleading look on her face to let her in. what the heck, one more sale before new years can't hurt, he thought to himself. he unlocked the door and let her in as she smiled brightly and said "thank you". "i'll just be a minute, i already know what i want to buy", she said. her hand pulled off a large bottle of vodka from the shelf and another bottle of bloody mary mix. "the register is closed miss, but being this is new years eve there will be no charge, its on me", he said with a smile. the young lady was very grateful and even kissed him on the cheek for her last minute purchase. she opened the front door and then turned back around with a questioning look on her face. maybe he read her mind and instinctively asked "do you have plans for tonight"? upon her shaking her head no he said "well, neither do i". at 11pm they arrived at her house from an invitation she gave him before leaving his store. there was a whole lot of conversation as they got to know each other just about 10 minutes before midnight. their favorite was served by her about a minute before the ball came down. they clicked glasses one minute into the new year and kissed for the first time. he whispered to stephanie the next morning on her pillow how much he loved her. she now shares a liquor store with her husband michael as they ring up the sales and receipts together. it was 10pm when she flipped the "open" sign to "closed". a chapter in their life from many pages to come...

the following june...

the dog barked outside a home in pennsylvania as stephanie rubbed her eyes and went outside to see what was going on. a man stood there petting the dog with one hand and holding a rose in the other. she held out her two arms and wrapped *them around his neck as they kissed for the first time. it was an unexpected visit from a buddy from another state who shared some dreams in e-mails they exchanged. she invited him in and put the rose in a vase on her kitchen table. the one week stay had them grow closer and a day before he was supposed to leave, they both stared at his return trip ticket to new York. he ripped it up in front of her with a questioning look in his eyes. she nodded yes with a smile as the question in his mind about staying there was answered. the dog licked both of their faces as they slept together that october night. under her pillow she felt something where one hand usually rested from a nightly habit. she opened the small black box to find an engagement ring that fit perfectly on her finger. the dog wagged its tail at a wedding the following June...*

a teen called audrey...

audrey was 12 years old waiting to become a teenager for the first time in her young life. it would be 6 months from now that the goal should be achieved. however the brain cancer with a diagnoses of 3 months to live had those hopes cut short. her biological parents had long since abandoned her when she was born and nobody really cared or thought about her. this article in the daily news touched me so deeply that i had to go to the hospital and see a perfect stranger who i knew nothing about. i told the receptionist that i was the godfather and she gave me a pass to the seventh floor where audrey lay dying. i held her hand and spoke softly to her as the little fingers gripped a little tighter around my fingers. she spoke to an angel while in the white light and He said "it is not your time, but could have been. a stranger has come and requested that you be with him". audrey opened her eyes just in time for her thirteenth birthday as a stranger smiled and cried. a make believe godfather had enough love and prayer to take her home with him. papers were signed and she became the official adopted daughter of a man who cared enough to bring her back to life. audrey inspired me to write this story as it is now printed in your heart....

i miss those days...

no lines to stand in, just a parking lot filled with cars at a drive in movie. i miss those days. pony tails and hula hoops with music that made sense and was easy to dance to. i miss those days. remember the good humor man in his white truck? he would reach behind the silver door and pull out a vanilla pop with sprinkles without even looking? where is my token that i used to drop in the turnstile to get to the train? card swiping has never been my thing. the breakfast section of the supermarket now has 500 different brands of cold cereals. do i need that much of a choice? i remember when it used to be corn flakes, rice krispies, and cheerios. that was all we knew and loved. i miss those days.

i still brush my teeth with the original tooth brush. i don't need an electric one that needs batteries or a plug in. my hand just works good enough. where are the parks and playgrounds where children don't get molested, young ladies don't get raped or mugged? never in my day when i was growing up, i miss those days. where are the payphones we used to drop a dime and a quarter into? all i see now are cell phones glued to the ears of people in a trance chatting about nothing. i wonder what happened to the letter i used to get in my mail box that was written in blue ink and had a stamp on the envelope. now i sit behind a computer and sort who is spam, who is lying, who is telling the truth. i miss those days. what's with earrings on guys, tattoos on girls, nose, eyes, and tongue piercing's? is there anybody out there who will join me at a drive in movie? i will pay for the tokens and give you a dime or quarter if you need to make a call. i love your pony tail by the way and may i have the next slow dance when music will be understood once again? i miss those days. we awoke with the thoughts and met at a simpler time. some angels agreed with us and dropped a quarter in a phone booth to let us know..

band-aids, old and new...

a painful paper cut that drew a little blood was covered with a band-aid by mom. four year old zelda never forgot that first instance of a healing as she grew to a mature twenty five year old young lady. mom had passed away and zelda wished that someone would heal the broken and torn relationships that followed her life into the early forty's. successful in business with a six figure income but no luck in keeping a boyfriend. the twenty five year old mail clerk delivered her mail at the office as usual, but this time a personal letter was included. it read something like this..."dear miss zelda, i have watched you get on the elevator to go home and you always have a sad look in your eyes. i know you make a lot of money so it cant be a bad financial state you are in. if you happen to be lonely and need a friend to talk to, then i am here for you. i may be a lot younger but i also experience the pain of not having someone. when i was four years old I had a painful paper cut that my mom fixed with a band-aid that i shall never forget. she is gone now, but maybe the healing still remains". zelda cried at the personal note and thought how he went through the exact same experience. age and circumstances didn't matter anymore as they dated and eventually became a couple. he placed an engagement ring on her finger as both moms smiled from up above. their wedding rings seem to resemble a band-aid with some healing powers that once was....

a season for mandy...

there is something about the seasons that affect us in our personal lives. winter seems to bring gloom and doom as the pretty colors of autumn brighten up our spirits. the first flowers and warmth of spring refreshes us in a way of almost being re-born again. summer brings us outdoors to beaches, pools, picnics, and barbeques. yet in those winter months we find something indoors called christmas and new years. to each his own in the joys and sorrows of seasons past and present. for mandy, the sadness was all year long as nobody was in her life that she longed to be with. she fed the pigeons from a park bench with a blank look in her eyes on a cold weekend in october. i sat next to her and fed them also. we held hands without knowing why and no words were spoken. maybe it was just something in our hearts that tried to bring our seasons together. we spoke of things that shared a common need and in the spring i sat next to her and handed mandy a rose. it was in the summer when we went to the beach and swam in pools. I poured the ketchup on her burger and she squeezed the mustard on my hot dog at our first barbeque together. there was something under the christmas tree in my living room for mandy. she opened the small black box and slid the engagement ring on her finger as she cried yes with tears. the following october was chilly in that park where we first met, yet there was a warmth as the outdoor wedding proceeded to take place. the guests flocked around as so did the pigeons for it was a season for mandy...

the following new years eve...

a seventeen year old runaway knocked on my door christmas eve. a torn pair of jeans and a ripped sweat shirt hid the heart of a broken soul. the wife and i welcomed her in as we wiped the black mascara that dripped with tears down her face. the young girl stuttered and stammered as we sat her down on the couch in our living room. the only identification was around her neck in the form of a gold chain with a name plate attached. her name was Susan. she sipped on the hot chicken soup that my wife had made and slowly told her story. we gave her a shower and tucked her in with fresh clothes as Susan slept comfortably for the first time. it was a strange coincidence that the wife and i lost a daughter in her childbirth some seventeen years before. we had planned to name her Susan. she awoke and talked about new years and how that was her birthday. the wife and i looked at each other and remembered that was the exact date when our daughter was supposed to be born. she had my nose and eyes and moms lips and ears. the resemblance scared us. in the voice of a little baby, susan asked " mommy, daddy"? we officially adopted her and the lost years were caught up in a miracle from God. the three of us blew out 18 candles the following new years eve...

as the ceremony continued...

she was the first one in class the next morning and smiled at the blackboard. an unknown admirer left his "i love you" the day before. grade school became high school and for graduation her parents bought her a brand new car. from a distance it looked like there was parking ticket on her windshield. she smiled at the note with the same hand writing and the same "i love you". while in college she became a part time bar waitress. beneath the empty beer bottle was a ten dollar tip and an "i love you" note on a brand new napkin. she scratched her head and tried to remember his face but couldn't. who is this mystery admirer that throughout the years he never shows himself? now at 31 years old she stood before an alter with a man she was about to marry. mom and dad thought he was the right one but she wasn't really in love. a stranger had his ear to the door as the priest said "is there anyone who objects to this marriage, speak now or forever hold your peace". the bride to be turned around as his screaming voice was heard beyond the church door. "I LOVE YOU"!!...she took his hand and smiled as chalkboards and parking tickets and notes on napkins suddenly became clear. a no longer secret admirer in his own rented tuxedo walked with her back to the alter as the ceremony continued....

for all humanity...

i helped an old lady cross the street as she said "thank you young man". a homeless person was given a hot cup of coffee with a bagel and cream cheese. he waved back at me with a tearful smile of "thanks for caring". the splint i fixed for a wounded bird with a broken wing recovered a few days later. the mother fed her daughter once again in a nest that was good to be back home again. she chirps a good morning to me on the way to work. a stray and undernourished cat filled her little belly with some food i had bought her. some months later she sleeps and purrs next to me on my bed. my time was up and an angel took me away. she helped me cross the heavenly street as i sipped on a hot cup of coffee and munched on a bagel with cream cheese. one of my arms became a wing and I felt like half an angel. she jumped on my pillow and purred as we slept in peace for all humanity...

burgers and hot dogs...

at the fast food window he ordered burgers and hot dogs. the young girl behind the glass slid two paper bags under the platform as he sat them on the seat of the passenger side of his car. it wasn't the food that brought him back often, but the smile on the face that said "hello, how may i serve you"? she left at 11 pm as usual when he honked his horn in the parking lot to get her attention. she walked *up to his car and said "hey, i remember you, a regular customer at least four times a week". "do you need a ride home"? he asked. "that would be nice, the bus usually takes a long time to get here", she replied. he dropped her off and asked for her phone number. a date was set up for a night that she was off from work. they went to a regular restaurant that neither had been to before. something on the menu happened to be a favorite of theirs as they ordered burgers and hot dogs. some ten years later after first dates have been forgotten, he drove to a restaurant and looked at the menu. just in front of him sat a familiar face. he walked over to her table and pointed at the menu and said, "may i recommend the burgers and hot dogs"? she smiled with a recognition of a first date long lost but not forgotten. "forget about that bus, let me drive you home", he said. a few months later two teens now in their early 30's made a commitment to each other. some 250 guests attended their wedding and opened the menu on the table where they sat. main course, burgers and hot dogs...*

she said with a smile...

somewhere in our brain or memory there is an event that never leaves us. time stands still for that special event. it was in another state at the age of five on a see-saw that rode up and down in a sandbox of a school long since forgotten. how can true love begin there at such a tender age. the only thing i remember about her was the name gail. it was on a sunday when the school was closed that i drove there and tried to re-capture a moment of time. my 35 year old legs pushed up and down as the sky came closer and closer. the weight on the other end had me even as i looked across the wooden plank and saw her holding on to the silver handle bars. from another state a 35 year old had the same memory of an event that stays with us for the rest of our lives. "hi, my name is gail", she said with a smile...

a pay phone, a dream...

she dropped a quarter in the pay phone from the bar she was working at. black mascara ran down her face as the phone in my hotel room rang. the loud music in the background didn't drown out the sobs on the other end and I knew she needed me. she stood outside the bar when my car came to a screeching halt as I reached over and opened the passenger door. it was just the loneliness that had her call and we drove down the long country highway until she spoke her feelings. carol was the bar waitress I met about a week ago and we shared a lifetime of heartaches and desires in a small town from Texas. we just kept driving until we left a state that needed to be forgotten. an abandoned car sat in the parking lot of the airport terminal as a jet took off for new york. I served her in my kitchen as she once served me in her bar. I dropped a quarter in a pay phone about one mile away from the church we were about to be married. "ill be there in five minutes" she replied. black mascara ran down her face and I kissed the tears of joy and then her lips at a wedding in new york...

no more notes...

it was the first rose in spring that i picked from my garden. i carefully wrapped it in cellophane and stapled a note to it. the box was shipped out with a delivery promise of three to five business days. your doorbell rang and you opened the box to smell the first scent of spring along with a note of the first hint of love. his name was someone that you remembered from a first romance in high school some thirty years ago. at a new years party a stranger walked in un-announced. he tapped on the shoulder of the man you were dancing with and cut in on a slow dance which you accepted. behind his back held in one hand was held a box with a scent of a spring for the second time. you unwrapped the cellophane and read the attached note. it was on a night table during the honeymoon where the vase sat there with a single red rose and no more notes....

"Karma"...

i am not a biology major but i believe women go to the bathroom more frequently than men. maybe not just to pee, but also to freshen up with some

143

perfume and make-up. in any case, lets get on with this story. it was down two flights of stairs where the long walk was to both men's and ladies room. maybe there was not enough seating in their room, I don't know, but what i did see was five women standing in line to get in. i did my business and came back out into the hallway of that popular bar and all of a sudden there were seven ladies on line. this didn't sit well with me knowing what its like when you have to go. our men's room had 3 stalls and at the present time it was empty. i waved the first three ladies in as i told them it was clear and safe. i stood watch and held one gentleman back from going in as i explained what i was doing. he laughed but agreed to my chivalrous gesture. all seven smiled on their way out and gave me a hearty thank you. four of them kissed me on the cheek which made me feel special and appreciated. some years later i re-visited this place and walked down those same long two flights of stairs. a sign read "out of order" taped to the men's room door. it was the girl from a few years ago who stood first on line that now tapped me on the shoulder. "my room is clear, i'll stand watch for you". i came out and kissed her on the cheek as we walked back up the stairs hand in hand. funny how karma has a payback. funny how the gold chain on her neck had engraved the name of this girl, "Karma"...

ladder 49...

joey tore away the wrapping from the christmas box that his mom had left underneath the tree. a shiny red fire truck with a pull up ladder and extendable hose was included. there was a rotating red light and a button that made a siren go off as he hugged and kissed mom. it was a toy that reminded the 10 year old of his dads passing as a first responder to the 911 attacks on the twin towers in manhattan. he labeled it with the decal "ladder 49", the official name of his dads truck. mom tucked her son in that night and they both went to sleep as usual. a lit cigarette toppled out of an ashtray and onto the living room rug. a neighbor saw the house caught fire and called 911. they rushed to the scene as the smoke subsided as mom and son stood outside the house, shaken but unharmed. one of the firemen stared at a red truck on the front steps of the house. its ladder was raised and a red flashing light blinked silently in the night. it siren shut off as he picked up the truck with a hose still dripping water from its nozzle. he opened the bottom only to find no batteries included. it made front page news about a miracle in a small neighborhood from new york. dad looked down and smiled from ladder 49.....

permanent this time...

she dusted off some items in the attic and found a book which she had read some thirty years ago.

her fingers peeled off the cellophane wrapper and she skimmed through the pages of memories long gone by. he went through some papers in his desk drawer and found a phone number with a star next to it from about thirty years ago. strange how two people discover items lost but recovered. she answered the phone while she held the book in her hand. "I missed a phone call before and would like to see you again", he said. a private meeting between the author and the reader was set to meet at her place. he had a pen in his hand to sign an autograph that was missed a long time ago. he was her hero back then at the age of fifteen and now age didn't really make a difference anymore. a marriage license was signed and the two of them had a signed autograph which became permanent this time...

a silent applause...

at seven years old she would sing along with the radio that would play music in our kitchen. pitch perfect and in tune with what was being heard. a natural talent at that age could not be wasted and so we sent her to a private music and voice instructor. stephanie took center stage in a musical play of "my fair lady", just before her graduation from grade school. she brought the house down with a thunderous round of applause and a standing ovation. a well known record company signed her to a contract while in her senior year of high school. these are my memories of what i treasured most. there was no college graduation for a week before a drunk driver left her lifeless body a few yards away from the house she was supposed to live in, my home. a few number one hits and a gold album sat pinned to the wall of her bedroom where she used to sleep. the seats and rows were empty now as i sat in the front row of madison square garden. one blue light lit up the stage and stephanie sang a song for her dad. it was a favorite one when old radios in a kitchen had dad and daughter dancing together. we smiled at each other from front row to stage as I gave a silent applause...in memory of my daughter Stephanie.

on the back of a bicycle...

the mansion had twenty five rooms and a two car garage with an outdoor swimming pool. across town the basement apartment had a living room, a kitchen, and a bathroom. each dwelling had two different single men, one poor one rich. the mansion had many guests but the owner eventually slept alone. the basement apartment had a young couple struggling trying to make ends meet. one counted his millions and the other counted his singles. a chauffeur drove him around town as the other had his girl on the back of his bicycle. happiness is in the eye of the beholder as caviar and Champagne versus beer and pretzels. i'll stay across town with you for love and companionship needs not twenty five rooms nor a two car garage. let me count my

single dollar bills as long as you are there with
me. i smiled and kissed you as my love rode on the
back of my bicycle....

for about twenty minutes...

the year was 1976 in the month of june. i was
about to meet my sister for a pre-celebration at
an italian restaurant in brooklyn, new york. she
and her groom to be sat at a table by the window
as a flat tire had me delayed for about twenty
minutes. bullets sprayed the window as a mob
boss went down in a hail of gunfire. three people
were killed instantly, the intended target and two
innocent civilians. i mourned the death of my
sister and her husband to be. some 30 years later
i drove down a block trying to re-live and change
the events of a past that had haunted me. i got out
my car before the flat happened and rushed into
the restaurant. "go quickly and leave now", i said
to my sister and her husband to be as they left
without a question. I sat beside the front window
and waited. a wedding took place where there
was not a delay for about twenty minutes...

on loves clock...

the waterfalls supplied the music to an outdoor
wedding at night somewhere in upstate new york.
a full moon and the bright stars lit the way under
a canopy where a slow dance took place after he
and she cut the cake. the clicking of glasses and

sound of crickets had the bride and groom kiss in a glow that was blessed by nature. frogs jumped from each lily pad on the lake to view the wedding ceremony as the uninvited guests croaked their approval. some fire flies lit the way for the guests departure as a honeymoon was only a tick away on loves clock...

that once was...

it was about an hour climb to the top of a mountain at a resort in pennsylvania. a place he once visited about thirty years ago. the memories of a clear blue sky with fresh mountain air and scenery was what took him back there. the hot july sun beat down between the branches of the trees as he rested and caught his breath from the long climb. the sound of familiar birds singing had him glance at the tree he was leaning up against. in the bark were initials carved with a pocket knife long since forgotten. he smiled and then remembered a first love at the age of twenty one. footsteps were heard behind him coming up a path that led to the top of a mountain. she looked over his shoulder and remembered what happened some thirty years ago. the birds sang a familiar tune as their lips met for a second time. he took out a new pocket knife and re-carved the initials that once was....

when it is time...

between the highest mountain and the deepest sea, she stood there waiting. somewhere between the north and south pole he stood there looking. maps and directions led to a place where maybe it was just a magnet of two lonely hearts. their fingers pushed the same floor button in an elevator where they both were supposed to be at a specific point in time. the waiting and looking were over as there is no distance or time when love is supposed to happen...

a gold chain, a heart...

if we ever met before or again, then take this chain with a heart and put it around your neck. she did so wondering why he said that but asked no questions. this was the event that happened to a middle aged couple who had met for the first time. at 61 and 59 they both felt like kids again and dated as such. they met online some months before and decided it was time to get together. the things in common were beyond coincidence as both were left handed. each had the same back problems diagnosed as a curvature of the spine with traces of arthritis. both were born at 6 AM and their profile picture was from the same year of 1981. the list goes on and on to the things that were common to both. time was short but they spent the next five years together before they passed away. a fifteen year old boy sat behind a thirteen year old girl in class one day. he saved up his allowance money from his parents over the last few months. she turned around from the seat in front of him as he put a gold chain around her neck with a heart...

without a bad goodbye...

the two eighth graders hugged at graduation. there was a smile saying between them that said without a bad goodbye. neither knew that they would meet again in high school. we dated during those four years until we hugged again at graduation, this time with a special kiss that said without a bad goodbye. she moved out of state and wrote from her college dormitory and i responded. the vietnam war had me drafted while she was a junior and we lost contact for a whole year. it was at her graduation that she thought she had seen a young soldier in the first row of the audience. he walked up to her but faded away with outstretched arms as unfinished business left her starring at her finger. the ring sparkled with a promise from the other side. he would wait for her until she joined him without a bad goodbye...

through stained glass windows...

the pastor gave his last sermon at the age of 35 and then left the church for no apparent reason. a dark and secret affair with a nun ten years his junior had his guilt drive him away to another state. at the age of 50 he returned to the now closed down and dusty house of worship where a bell sits still and quiet. he dusted the cobwebs off the pulpit from where he used to speak. his speech was silent in prayer asking for forgiveness as the morning sun shone through the foggy stained glass windows. the front door creaked open and a 40 year old lady sat in the last row and prayed for forgiveness. the figure on the cross that stood on a wall watched intently and shed a tear of understanding and compassion. a storm outside crackled and thundered for a moment until the sunrise peeked through the now clear stained glass windows. he was 35 again and the 25 year old held his hand in a proper ceremony that should have taken place, but will do for now. the figure on the cross smiled as sins of the past were forgiven and now made right again in a time where second chances shine through stained glass windows...

cowboy hats and sawdust...

a small club about a mile from the motel had a sign outside. "live band Wednesday and Saturday". it sat just outside of fort worth, texas. they knew i wasn't a local as soon as i walked into the bar. my white shirt and a tie must have been a clue. a corner table was empty and i tried to stay away from the starring eyes that seem to snicker at me. the waitress kicked up some sawdust on the floor as she approached me in her brown leather boots and cowboy hat. "hey stranger, what's your pleasure"? she asked. "a pitcher of beer and maybe some friendly faces", i replied. the regulars danced as i just tapped my feet to the music and watched. the band took a break and my waitress said, "I'm on a break now also, wanna help me pick a song on the jukebox"? i recognized a big hit from back east and suggested "the rose" by bette midler. "good choice, feel like dancing?" she asked with a shy smile. she placed her cowboy hat on my head and i suddenly felt like i fit in with the rest of the crowd. eyes looked at us together but this time they seemed a lot more friendly. we ended back in my motel room and talked for quite a few hours about each other. still dressed, we both fell asleep in each others arms. she felt like a stranger back east where she moved in with me but one dance from a jukebox made her feel at home. some guests wore white shirts and ties as others wore brown leather boots and cowboy hats. the wedding hall had sawdust on the floor as friendly eyes got up and joined the bride and groom for a slow dance...

black and white, to color...

there was an old black and white photo that sat beneath a park bench. i reached down and picked it up to see a young man and his wife standing next to each other with a baby in her arms. i took it home to mom and she looked at it cried. she sat me down and told me a long story of how her husband left her shortly after the baby was born. the single mom who gave birth to me and raised me all these years had just revealed my long lost dad. my twenty fifth birthday was on *christmas eve when the doorbell rang as mom and I exchanged gifts. the old man looked at me and reached out with forgotten arms as mom did the same. time lost was made up in a reunion that was found under a park bench so many years ago. there was an old black and white photo that now was in color....*

a few years later...

we passed the time by playing checkers, chess, and card games. in between we would sit and stare at the old television hanging up on the wall in the recreation room. some of us would walk out on crutches and others would be pushed from a wheelchair. either way was followed by a blue and white capsule with a small cup of water that had us sleep through the night. michael was 98 and carol was 94. she moved a checker only this time he noticed a gold ring with a blue stone on her finger. he took out his magnifying glass and said "may i look at that ring please"? the date was 1965, the year he graduated high school. "carol, think back and look at me now", he said with a wrinkled smile. nobody saw them leave together and the old age home was missing two files on two patients that once were there. an 18 year old and a 14 year old freshman held hands and kissed for the second time. a second chance, a second life. time lost was found once again this time a few years later the ring was gold with a diamond chip. she said yes....

hand written...

mass e-mails floated back and forth to groups and individual members. some are read, some deleted, some responded to, some just forgotten. in a world of computer communication something was being sought after by this one particular writer. it was an old idea of one on one thoughts and feelings. like we used to do with some note paper folded in three where blue ink was used by a pen and signed. an envelope with a stamp sent it on its way. maybe its time to leave the house and go to a nice quiet library. a tap on my shoulder had me turn around as she said "remember me? you signed your book incredible short stories last month for me at the new york public library." the one on one conversation continued which i never heard or felt before. a real live person stood before me as we both took out a pen with blue ink and jotted down each others phone numbers. strangely enough we folded the note paper three times, something that was remembered from a while back. our computers were logged off and shut down as we hand wrote the invitations to our wedding....

the next barbeque...

two grills were running at the same time in my backyard as guests marched into 500 square feet of free space. the smell of burgers and hot dogs and chicken wings filled the air with an aroma of anticipation. tables sat at the four corners of the yard with hot corn on the cob, salads, coleslaw, baked ziti, meatballs, and fresh french fries and broiled potatoes. an open bar with wine and beer and 15 brands of mixed drinks was available. soda and fruit punch was there for the kids. two bathrooms, one on the main floor and one upstairs had the traffic going back and forth. it was a comfortable 72 degrees outside and the piped music from four speakers echoed the favorite oldies from pre-recorded cassette tapes. a full moon lit up the backyard along with colored lanterns scattered about the perimeter. the guests left a few at a time as the night wore down to just about midnight. you fell asleep on the hammock that was swinging between two trees. I walked and carried you to the guest spare room and tucked you in. "thank you for letting me spend the night, is there anything I can do before I leave"? we both cleaned up from the night before and then you looked at me with wondering eyes. you stayed over for the rest of the weekend and the following year there was another barbeque. you flipped burgers on one grill and i rolled the hot dogs on the other. only difference this year was something that was printed on the mailbox just outside the backyard. MR. & MRS....

come take my hand...

come take my hand for a little trip to a hotel in upstate n. y. it was owned by my uncle and the *following years of my growing up there during the summer months. from 1950 to 1964 we shall be there together as i describe what was remembered. you will live, breath, and feel the same experiences as i did so let us begin the journey. it starts with the tires of a car crunching over the gravel in the main parking lot. mom and dad go to the front desk and pick up the key to our room. on the wall is posted the days and nights activities of what to do and where to go. bingo night is on Wednesday and Friday has a movie in the casino as Saturday has a comedian or magician to entertain us. the baseball field had me hit my first home run as you cheered from the sidelines. further away was the campgrounds where we roasted marshmallows and hot dogs as the camp counselor told ghost stories. sunday afternoon we would go to indian waterfalls and catch salamanders beneath the rocks in a shallow pond. we would bring them home to mom and dad in an old empty coffee can with a lid that had holes punched in so they can breath. come take my hand..our last year together was in 1964, one year before my uncle died and the hotel closed down. we looked at each other in a different light as growing up from children to adults at 24 and 20. it was on the stage in a casino where the magician once performed his magic. we kissed for the first time. the hotel is now under different management as our tires crunched over the gravel in the main parking lot. come take my hand....*

the lake was quiet and calm...

the lake was quiet and calm when we slowly paddled beneath the stars. a light wind blew the leaves that august night as the crickets sang in the background. you stood up in the canoe out of excitement when i pulled out a ring and asked you to marry me. a wrong balance and slip broke the silence of a still lake when you went fell overboard. your outstretched hand surrounded bubbles that i could never recover. the ring fell from my hand as the lake swallowed up my heart and soul. the leaves stop blowing and the crickets stopped singing. that was end of a summer in 1947. michael drove his 1977 convertible back to a resort of forgotten and suppressed memories. a strange mist of a cabin appeared on the shore that wasn't there before. a figure of a young woman opened the door and waved at him. instinct with no conscious thought had him row to shore and meet her before she got into the canoe to meet him. he placed a ring on her finger and asked her to marry him. just outside the entrance was a 1947 ford which they both got into and drove on to their wedding and eventual honeymoon. the lake was quiet and calm when we both paddled beneath the stars. a light wind blew the leaves that august night as the crickets sang in the background...

midtown elevator...

looking out the train window we stared at each other as one went uptown and the other downtown. it was a first impression without actually having met before. there came a time when both of us got off the train to see each other beyond a pane of glass. we talked for a minute or two before the next hour had us both late for work that morning. the next few weeks were empty without having seen her across the platform. all we knew of each other was a first name and a quick kiss on the cheek before we got on our respective train ride to work. a company layoff had me unemployed for a few months until i found another job in midtown. it was in the elevator that she got on and pressed the same floor as mine. seems fate had her laid off also as she found her new job in midtown. we have lunch together now every day and ride the same train back and forth to work. our last names were revealed. in the spring that year i proposed to her in a midtown elevator where everybody got off on our floor and applauded and cheered. uptown and downtown through a window on a train was where it all began. it ended and still lives on in a midtown elevator...

i don't do windows...

the 23 year old maid entered my office as usual after hours at about seven o'clock that evening. she felt a breeze from the half open window and knew something wasn't right. Maria walked to the window and saw me sitting on the ledge looking down some 45 stories below. her broken English with a heavy Spanish accent screamed out at me as the bottle of vodka fell from my hand. I turned around and said "now look what you done, who's going to clean up this mess"? she waved her finger back and forth as if to say "no, don't do it". the maid raised her hand and said "wait one minute, I have something for you". she came back with some coffee from the vending machine just outside my office. just what I needed, some coffee to sober up before I jumped. she laughed and then I laughed as the young maid wiped the tears from my face and then held my hand. "you are going to catch your death of cold sitting out here on the ledge" she said with a straight face. I almost peed in my pants from laughing so hard as she helped me back into the office while she then closed the window. maybe it was someone who finally cared and made me laugh again. I put her through secretary school and then hired her as my personal guardian angel. a now happy 40 year old vice president looked at life and her a lot different now. I announced our engagement at the following company xmas party where Maria and i finally got married. it was on the ground floor at our wedding ceremony where she took away my vodka and served me coffee as she closed a half open window. our laughter echoed throughout the hall as our honeymoon produced a lovely baby girl. at five years old she told her mom and dad "I don't do windows"...

FIRST DATE...

in a world of computer make believe, the two of them set up a date night. it was for every Friday from 4 pm to 5 pm. they would exchange chat as usual but this time each had a drink sitting on a snack table next to the monitor. "cheers hun", he would type and "cheers my darling", she would reply. a midi file of a slow song was played through each others head phones as they danced together in their minds in between the typing. he would take her to different places every friday and they went there together from each side of the monitor in a dream that seemed so very real. she met him in person as all of the above became a reality. kiss + hug happened instead of words on a keyboard, now for real. they saw each other every Friday, for now date night was face to face. in the month of june she became his bride somewhere between 4 pm to 5 pm. the cover of their wedding album had a beautiful photo of a kiss just after the priest pronounced them man and wife. in bold capital letters on the album cover, read "FIRST DATE"...

under the stars...

June 10, 1958...a marshmallow roast and hot dogs on the end of pointed long twigs sat over a campfire. it was under the stars that a twelve year boy and an eleven year girl held hands as the camp counselor told ghost stories. during the day they would meet at the outdoor swimming pool and laugh and play together. their lips met under the pool water and two giggles had some bubbles rise to the top. they held hands while watching cartoons and thought about each other before going to sleep. these events surfaced in my memory many years later. June 10, 1988...a forty two year old man went back to the campgrounds of a hotel where he had once been before. i found a long pointed twig and roasted a hot dog under the stars. i didn't hear the footsteps behind me as a forty one year lady said "that sure smells good, mind if i join you"? we held hands and knew a familiar touch from years gone by. our lips met under the stars...

a special delivery...

she stood outside my front door wearing a red cap and white blouse with pink stripes. i took the pizza pie from her hands and placed it on the kitchen table and returned to her with a two dollar tip. that's how it was every friday night during the summer of 1971. i was twenty three back then and my guess she was about seventeen. there was something that smiled in her eyes which told me something more than just a delivery. september came and there was a knock on my front door. she stood there in her regular street clothes and told me she had just been laid off from her job. "come in for a while and let's talk", i said. we knew each other by first name only and the time came to know a little more. being a young manger at a department store had its benefits as i offered her a position in my department. her teary eyes smiled once again as a warm and tender hug took place. we spent xmas and new years together as the following summer she moved in with me. i paid off a clerk at the local jewelry store to have something delivered to our apartment. the timing was perfect on her birthday when the bell rang and i asked her to please answer the door. "special delivery from j&m jewelry shop", the clerk said. she opened the little box while walking towards me with a look of surprise. i slid the ring on her finger and said "happy birthday hunny". some co-workers from the department store and a few loyal friends from a pizza shop attended our wedding. a red cap and white blouse with pink stripes. a loving smile and a special delivery...

as hot buttered popcorn...

the scent of the salt water crashing on the sands of the beach below the boardwalk. the sounds of the rides with children laughing and screaming in the distance. hot dogs and fries with burgers and pink cotton candy as hot buttered popcorn fills the air. it comes from a place called coney island in brooklyn, new york. my new car pulled up and parked into an old space where it once sat. most of the rides were still there as the people had come back like i did to recapture our childhood. it was in the tunnel of love, a ride where most youngsters held hands and kissed for the first time that i found myself sitting in alone. when the ride was over my dad and mom helped me and my first girlfriend out of the car. she must have parked her car next to mine somewhere in the future. we held hands and kissed again even though i'm not sure whether we were adults or just kids. it didn't really matter though for we were together again. it was on the sand just below the boardwalk where the scent of salt water crashing where we said our vows. the guests sat at their tables with hot dogs and fries with burgers and pink cotton candy as hot buttered popcorn fills the air...

together again...

8 pounds and 7 ounces, 22 inches long. i looked through the glass window as the nurse held him up. in the blink of eye i was pitching a baseball at him as the 9 year old swung his bat. i stood behind him as he marched down the isle at 23 with his bride to be. that was my last memory of him when a stray bullet from a drive by shooting took his life. his room remained the same with some favorite toys and a teddy bear that i used to tuck him in with. a ball, a bat, and a glove sat still beside the foot of his bed. my time came when he was there to greet me on the other side. he threw the ball and my bat swung a home run. the nurse looked from beyond a window and saw us together again....

before the thunder storm...

we held hands in a drive in movie during a thunder storm when the picture and sound were cut off. the only car remaining was ours as we created our own images and voices. last call at the bar some years later left us standing in the parking lot dancing to a tune where we held each other close just an hour before. remember when i walked you home carrying your school books? remember our first phone call that lasted over an hour? oh, the little details of our lives that had me fall in love with you. your eyes said yes with tears as your fingers opened a little black box with a shiny ring that i put on your trembling finger. it was then and now that i hold you close and dance and sing and love again. the priest didn't blink an eye as the thunder storm shut off power and we said our vows. remember the little girl born unto us before the thunder storm? i love you then and now and forever and always....

the drive in movie...

the parking lot was still there but now stood a shopping mall which used to be a drive in movie. i just sat in my car and reflected back to a time of precious memories. a girl on roller skates would knock on the window and serve fast food as the outdoor microphone hung inside my car. a few fries and wrappers from two burgers sat between us in the front seat as we held hands. there was *a kiss and a hug and promises of being together always. a simple time when love was not that complicated. my radio suddenly played oldies music as the 2,008 chevy suburban became a 1964 ford mustang. a girl on roller skates knocked on my window...*

a january rose...

a january rose was a gift given out of season, yet the timeless essence of its meaning had a significant impact to the one it was given to. it was the first rose of her receiving and my first rose of giving so who knew of seasons and flowers? her wedding dress matched the color of a reddish pink gift that she got about a year ago. the band played a slow wedding song as we danced to a bette midler tune called the rose. a poem was copied into our album which i had written and later became the inspiration for a love novel called a january rose...

to catch a butterfly...

to catch a butterfly, that was what it was like to watch twelve year old melissa dance. she would float and flutter across the stage in her golden ballet slippers. her thirty minute performances at each of her concerts had the full house standing on its feet, applauding, cheering, whistling and wanting an encore performance. i was her agent and also her dad. those golden slippers still sit in her bedroom where she never saw her thirteenth birthday. on the anniversary of her passing i sit on her bed each year and watch those ballet shoes move about the floor, no proof needed to show others, just a happy dad that knows she still comes around as i stand and applaud, and whistle. my butterfly has landed...

a robot named desire...

a robot named desire. she was a product that came from the year 2,020 that was programmed to clean house, cook, and do general household functions. she was fitted with a uniform, skin color, eye color and every other feature to fit your personal needs. her name was personally selected by me as i thought it to be appropriate. After about a month or two i became sort of attached to this object of metal and wires and circuits that made me feel there was something more than household chores. she would play checkers and chess and a few card games with me that gave a sense of more than just winning and losing. her blue eyes would sadden when i would lose and her lips would smile when i had won. a robot named desire. i would feel the blanket cover me as i slept but knew not why. the sound of shattered glass had her run to the front door window as she fought off a break-in intruder, defending our home. i cried the next day as model 1464 was carted off to be fixed and maybe repaired in a shop some miles away. i placed an ad in the newspaper for a real live housecleaning maid as she knocked on my door. her blue eyes smiled at me and her lips looked like they were ready to be kissed. maybe metal and flesh have a way of coming together with a human and a robot named desire...

breakfast in cabin 12...

the logs in the fireplace were still burning that dark december morning. he picked up the phone and order breakfast for cabin number 12 at a resort in the pocono mountains. the joined cabins with thin walls heard some crying and sobbing next door. he knocked on cabin number 11 and looked at her face of depression as he wiped a tear from her eye. "feel like company this morning? i just ordered breakfast which should be here in a few minutes." he didn't remember why he made a double order that morning, but it came anyway to cabin number 12. she lit the fireplace that evening when her hand wiped a tear from his eye. thin walls heard cries from the heart and responded accordingly. it was the following july when they shared cabin number 12 a few hours before their wedding...

a few inches from heaven...

his trembling hand unwrapped the gift he left for himself under a half decorated xmas tree. it snowed outside the basement apartment window when the middle aged man twisted off the cap to his favorite bottle of cologne. its scent had reminded him of happier times when it used to be a gift from someone he lost in earlier years. her trembling hand unwrapped the gift she left for herself under a half decorated xmas tree only a few blocks away. the middle aged woman twisted off the cap to her favorite bottle of perfume. its scent had reminded her of happier times when it used to be a gift from someone she lost in earlier years. somewhere in between their houses a few blocks from each other it was new years eve. the liquor store had two last customers who once knew each other but each failed to remember the other. it was trembling hands a few blocks away that squeezed off one shot under a lonely half decorated tree from a week before. tears of an angel fell from the top down as the snow subsided a few inches from heaven....this short story is a message to the depressed who have no where to turn. be strong and love life. lets decorate the tree again as i give you perfume and you give me cologne. love, michael.

after hours...

the windows on the second floor of the after hours bar were painted black. no sunlight came in the early morning hours as the perpetual night time was just a temporary prison of lost souls trying one last time to meet that special someone. the fantasy became a reality when the two of us sat at a table for two in an all night diner. from there it led to one of our apartments where passion and love had happened for the very first time. it was a rented hall about a year later where the bride kissed the groom. then in a hospital room a little girl was born on the second floor. in their present house there were no black windows, just a view of life that happened after hours...

initials and hearts...

it was in the summer of 1998 in a small but cozy restaurant that i ordered pork fried rice with an egg roll and wonton soup. an ordinary night as usual until i went to pay the bill at the front register. on her shoulder was a tattoo with initials m.r. and a heart beneath it. like a bolt of lightening i was brought back to 1968 in vietnam where a love that was forgotten was shot back to me in the present time. mei ling was her name and her initials m.l. with a heart beneath it rested on my shoulder. we both stared at each other and remembered. she waved to the waitress who served me, our 31 year old daughter. the wedding took place with our daughter cutting the cake for mom and dad that was missing but now was found. initials and hearts once engraved again where things were supposed to be all along...

enemy of mine...

an enemy of mine was sleeping next to an open wallet behind a tree that stood in front of me. this german soldier held a pistol in one hand and a half lit cigarette in the other as no more gunfire was heard, just the chirping of crickets. it was the end of world war two but we never heard the radio announce it. i picked up his open wallet to see a photo of his wife and two children that he was obviously was looking at before the sleep of this tireless war took its tool. it was the same picture that sat in my wallet which reminded me of times of love and peace and family. he abruptly woke up and pointed his pistol at my head and shouted in a language I did not understand. gently my hand held his photo in front of his face as i then showed him mine. it was also of a wife and two children and his expression of hate changed to something of what compassion used to be . we couldn't understand each other's words but somehow gestures made sense. he laid the pistol to the ground and offered me a smoke as flyers rained down from the skies above that the war was over. we saw each other in civilian clothes the following year on neutral grounds where there was no longer an enemy of mine...

a classmate of mine...

debbie was a classmate of mine from grammar school to high school to college. it seemed i was her big brother and protector through those tender years where others would laugh and make fun of her braces, her glasses, her hair, the way she dressed, and so on and so forth. she was a kind hearted soul who never hurt anybody but would always be hurt. why are others so quick to judge and make fun of those who do not meet their standards? one night after work we met for dinner and she opened a little black box that contained an engagement ring. i fixed her fallen glasses that fell off of her face and placed them back gently on the bridge of her slightly crooked nose. "debbie, will you marry me?" i asked. her heart smiled behind the silver braces of a smile that had long since been forgotten. it was three years later that my beauty queen won the miss America pageant. debbie was a classmate of mine..

a ring remembered...

it was on a beach where i used to hang out at with my high school sweetheart. the place was coney island in the borough of brooklyn. that was back in 1965 when I placed my high school graduation ring on her finger. that memory had me go back there some twenty years later to find why a love was taken from me by an accidental drowning. the waves crashed upon the sand under a full moon as it did before. i stepped on a small metal object and picked it up from the top of my blanket. it was a high school ring with a blue stone that read "mid wood high school, 1965." engraved in the back was "to my sweetheart gail." the tides turned backwards as so did the years when i stood there with a ring held about to be put on her finger. this time around i told her not to go in the water. it was a second chance that most of us never have and some twenty years later we live and love together as a married couple in the borough we used to grow up in. chalk it up to angels that guide our destiny with sands and waves and a full moon that shined on a high school ring where love never dies...

up the down staircase...

there she was, riding the down escalator as i was going up. our heads turned around at the same time and we both wanted to say something. we never spoke as the crowd and our place of where we needed to go had that moment slip away. we missed other but rode the same elevator on different schedules in the same building where each of us worked. strangers who at a glance wanted to meet up the down escalator. we spun together in a revolving door as she was coming in and i was leaving and it was then that each of us turned around for the second time. we met outside the lobby in the street and just looked at each other with thoughts of "do i know you? or "have we met before"? our eyes met and somewhere in the pit of our heart and soul we knew that it was our time to be together. in a hall that was rented for a wedding about a year later we both walked up the down staircase. we ride and walk together now where heads sometime turn around for a brief moment. it is then that the moment and purpose of why we are here becomes clear. a lesson on love that almost escaped up the down staircase.

an angels message...

the plane was flying too low as i could see water and buildings out of the window seat. it picked up speed and then an explosion, darkness followed by a light where we the passengers walked toward with the help of the flight attendants. our final destination was reached but not from a ticket that we all had purchased. remember our cell phone conversation just before the impact? there were many angels and guides waiting for us that morning of september eleventh on both the ground and in the air. my name is michael and i just wanted to let you know that we are all alright now and still alive, just in a different place. we send subtle messages to those we left behind through scents of our cologne or perfume. sometimes a bird taps or flies by your window. you may find pennies on the floor in your home where they are not expected to be found. maybe the smell of a favorite food has entered the kitchen when you are not cooking. or maybe a faint voice whispers a message on the answering machine. i have never left you as your dreams i will enter once again.... dedicated to the memory of those lost and yet to be found again where the bonds of love and friendship shall always be there.

tender are the eyes...

tender are the eyes that cry and mourn. tender are the eyes that smile and laugh and rejoice. the *blind see with their heart and those who have vision ignore what is before them. look at me from a distance and know that i am close to you. tender are the eyes...*

a toast to remember...

he held the cork screw tightly as it popped the champagne cork from its green bottle. it was one minute before the new year when in a dark alley behind his apartment she twisted off the bottle cap from a beer. his television showed the ball come down as her portable radio gave announcements of the event. the only common thing was both were alone. through his open window cries and sobbing was seen as a tear of his own fell on the alley below. his footsteps went down the stairs and she turned around to see him there with two glasses held in each hand for a toast caught in the middle of two different worlds. the newspapers burnt out from the garbage can which had the fire that kept her warm. he took her hand and they walked upstairs where the homeless and the well off become one and the same. loneliness on two different conditions was the same, but not anymore. the television and her radio played the same theme as beer bottle and champagne clicked in the new year. love found a halfway point between a stair case and an alley where he and she never shed another tear.

the last unwrapped gift...

tommy unwrapped his last gift under the xmas tree. the 10 year old hugged and kissed his mom while holding a red toy model of a firetruck which was a dream come true. his single mom tucked him into bed and he played with it under the covers until he fell asleep. new years eve crept up shortly after xmas as a retired fireman knocked on her door. he was in full uniform as she stared at the man who left her eleven years ago. he just stood there with nothing to say but the tears running down his face said it all. she took his hand and led him into the bedroom where he saw his son for the first time. "i have ten years of missing time. is it too late to catch up?" mom woke up their son as he starred at the retired fireman and said "daddy"? they got to know each other and mom and dad became what it used to be. tommy played ball and got help with homework the following year with the dad who he had never known. mom laughed some twenty years later when her husband was sleeping under the xmas tree. a big red bow was tied around his father as a red firetruck sat on his lap. the last unwrapped gift...

to feel, to see...

to feel, to see...a loved one has passed on and they may have been 80 or 15 years old. what do they have common? they both have completed their time here and learned life's lessons in order to move on to the other side. they leave us subtle signs like pennies to be found in a place where it is not likely to be. a song on the radio reminds us of them or the smell of cologne or perfume lingers in a room where they once lived. the bond has always been there and always will be as life and death are just but a continuous circle of where we have been and where we have re-visited. if i rang a bell in your heart and soul then smile. for it is something to feel, to see…

and so the mind of a child…

and so the mind of a child sits in the head of my 61 year old body. i lost a tooth and put it under my pillow just out of habit and belief. sure enough the tooth fairy left a dollar bill there the next morning. i built a snowman outside my front porch on xmas eve just before i decorated the tree inside my living room. of course there would be no presents since I lived alone, but i still made a secret wish to santa. the next morning there was a card under the tree. it read "meet me when the bell rings at ten am. i opened the front door as a 59 year old lady stood there with just a smile on her face. she told me of how a tooth was left under her pillow and was replaced by a dollar bill. then she pointed to a snow woman that sat beside a snowman on my front porch. we sat together for a while in my living room and then went to hers. she showed me a card under her xmas tree which read "meet me when the bell rings at 11am. it was new years eve

*when we wished each other a happy new year.
there sat two people who were now 21 and 19.
maybe its just a habit or a belief, who really knows
for sure? and so the mind of a child...*

g.w. & l.f. forever...

*some names resurfaced from two past lives
remembered. they both felt the connection without
logic or reason, it just happened that way. they
were gray wolf and little fawn, husband and wife
from an old american indian heritage they once
shared. it was time to meet again as she drove
some five hours to where he lived. a hug and kiss
was long awaited when they met in person for
the first time. they talked as if they knew each
other forever. in this life there were so many
things in common as it was before. music, food,
drinks, hobbies, clothes, etc, etc. they traveled to
the catskill mountains in upstate new york where
he been before as a child. it was a place he used to
take hikes up a special path to a mountain above.
they held hands and walked and climbed between
the trees and the sun above. she said "this place
looks so familiar to me, have we been here before"?
just at the top of the mountain stood a tree all by
itself. it was as fresh as it was over two hundred
years ago. in the bark was initials carved from the
past now in the present. g. w. & l. f. forever....*

A Halloween angel...

The children rang the bell and said at the same time "trick or treat". I handed them each a variety of candy bars along with a dollar bill. Familiar moms waved back at me as they did each year when they walked their kids through the neighborhood. There was a little girl who seemed to play peek-a-boo from behind a tree just across the street. She was dressed as a little angel with wings and a halo attached to her head. I wondered why she never rang my bell. The night flew by and it was 9 PM as almost all of the kids had been taken home by their parents. My bag of treats was empty and the 50 single dollar bills were spent wisely once again on children who appreciated that extra little something. I turned out the lights in my kitchen as she stood there across the street waving at me from behind a tree. My better judgment told me to go outside and talk to this little girl about going back home to her parents house. It was too late now for kids to be outside by themselves. Her wings fluttered when her arms moved up and down, yet their was no arms. A halo had no visible support to her head as it glowed in front of me. She took my hand and walked me back home without saying a word. It was a different home from what I was used to. A place I originally came from. And so an angel who takes on many forms, sometimes as a child, walked with me to where I was supposed to go to...

to the sound of a waterfall...

the guests consisted of those who lived there. birds, crickets, raccoons, fish, and whoever else dwelled in the forest. there was no live band, just the music of a waterfall nearby. it was a ceremony where no priest was needed, just two people who give and accept a ring in a non traditional wedding. whether it be legal or recognized by the state didn't really matter to them. nature blessed the bride and groom as they kissed under the stars with a full moon as their witness. man made laws need not apply to matters of the heart. a rented cabin was a place of their honeymoon in the middle of a forest. they slow danced and made love to the sound of a waterfall...

bang the drum slowly...

i picked up two pencils and tapped on a cardboard box while the radio was playing. mom and dad noticed how i kept a steady beat with the music as they thought their 5 year old son may have a hidden talent. at 13 i got my first drum set as it was set up in the basement of our house. i would play along with the music from a radio that had a microphone next to it. at 17 i became a member of a band where i was the drummer and we stayed together for 5 years. my parents showed me a photo of great, great grandpa as he was the drummer during the civil war. maybe it was inherited in my genes. bang the drum slowly. my *second band lasted another 10 years as we played in different clubs in many cities and states. we never made the big time, but did rack in on the money and had a small group of devoted fans. our last performance was at a sweet sixteen party where the girl who was honored and i became very close. she showed me photos of her family as a great, great grandfather was put out before me. he stood next his american indian wife before he joined the civil war. bang the drum slowly. maybe it was in the genes that we had something in common. we lost touch for a while but reunited some years later at an oldies club which brought back some fond memories. where the wedding took place didn't really matter. we kissed and said our vows as with no live band present. maybe it was the sound toms toms that beat in our hearts to begin with. bang the drum slowly...*

the yellow rose...

she opened her high school year book to capture some old memories. next to her photo was a faded yellow rose with a greeting card. it read "let us never loose touch with each other, i love you now and forever". that was some thirty years ago but she cried the same tears now as once before. his old photo was next to hers as if they never left each other. she sat quietly in a single booth at a restaurant which was a regular place attended over the weekend. the waiter brought her dinner as usual, but when she came back from the ladies room, there was a yellow rose sitting in a vase in the middle of the table. a card sat there also with the words "let us never loose touch with each other, i love you now and forever". the waiters face was a lot older now but the look in his clear blue eyes was the same. they drove home together to her house and talked about old times. i opened an old wedding album of mom and dad some thirty years later. their photos were on the same page with a faded yellow rose and a card that read "let us never loose touch with each other, i love you now and forever".

in return...

the poem or story was read and absorbed. she wondered in her mind if this pertained to her or was it just for the general public at large. there was a thought or item or place that made it personal for her. it felt like a rose on her doorstep. the other recipients of maybe about a hundred or so took it at face value. when she had dreams about him, then she knew it was for her. there was a surprise visit as a knock on his door awoke him one Saturday morning. she stood there with a rose in her hand and smiled at him. it was her presence that responded alive and in person in the form of a poem and a story that was only meant for him in return.

november fifteenth...

the meeting was planned some months earlier and now it came down to ten days away. their mail and chats had intensified along with both dreaming of this event. this special connection between two hearts was soon to be a reality. she packed her car for a four day stay at his place and then filled up the gas tank for a five hour drive. a well needed nap was taken after three hours of being on the road. a pit stop for food and drink and a few freshen up needs were taken care of. the black ford taurus rode down white plains road and she knew that only in a few minutes she would be there. lincoln ave was up ahead as she turned left. it was a little earlier than the time they were supposed to meet, so she sat in her car and waited for him to walk out into the street. his head turned left and right as he heard the sound of a car honking its horn. she got out of the vehicle and waved at him. it seemed to be in slow motion as the two walked towards each other. they called out each others name and then hugged and kissed like there was no tomorrow. hand in hand this couple walked into the complex where he lived. november fifteenth was a day and night to be remembered. the feelings and emotions that once was through a computer now became real. her black ford taurus sat in his driveway longer than expected. you see, the four days now became four months. it wasn't a popular time of year for weddings in general, but for them it was. a seven and a half ring size sat on her finger from when they met. it was meant to be that they would be together. i took the photos at their wedding this year of 2,008 november fifteenth....

slipping on ice...

it was the third time she slipped on the ice when i picked her up back to her feet. "maybe we should skate together"? she said as we both laughed out loud. tired ankles and sore rear ends had us take off our skates as the good old fashion way of walking again was a blessed relief. we walked into the underground bar-restaurant just below street level in Rockefellers rink in the heart of N. Y city. the both of us kicked off our shoes and wiggled our toes to make sure they were still alive. she sipped on a wine and I sipped on my beer as we talked and got to know each other. after dinner we decided not to end this perfect evening. neither one of us drove into the city that xmas, so it was just a matter of which train we would take back to one or the others apartment. love finds each other slipping on ice and may iI say it was well worth the bumps and bruises. the photographer took wedding pictures from above the rink and also below as the december event was a place that would be remembered forever. our now 23 year old son visited a place where his mom and dad first met. it was the third time she slipped on the ice when he picked her up back to her feet...

a playground remembered...

it started in a playground during the years of grade school. innocence holding hands and kissing each others cheek. high school had two familiar faces recognize each other from a while back as they next kissed on the lips. she wore his graduation ring until they each departed for different colleges in different states. time erases memories and until they met again. he was looking for an engagement ring for nobody in particular, but wanted it just in case. the lady behind the counter showed him the best that there was. he noticed a gold ring with a blue stone on her finger that was placed so, so many years ago. "Michael?, is that you?, she said with a familiar look in her eyes. he nodded his head yes as tears rolled down his cheeks. a kiss on the cheek and then on the lips over the counter where time caught up with them again. "i'll take this ring please" he said to her. "and who is the lucky lady"? she said with a smile. customers and other shoppers watched the event take place as a round of applause echoed through the store. michael placed it on her finger and she said yes, i do. the old neighborhood was still there as well as the playground where they first met. the bride and groom slid down a slide. they kissed on the cheek and then on the lips at a place where we all long to be...

Michael Reisman

when the leaves would change colors...

dad left my mom before i was born. when i was 13 she explained the best way she could the circumstances of his leaving. it didn't make sense to me but i had to accept it as a fact of life. at 25 i would often go to the park on weekends, especially during the fall season when the leaves would change colors. an old man sat on a park bench where he fed the pigeons and sipped on a cold cup of coffee. he waved at me when i walked by on my way to work. we talked a few times and i shared some hot bagels and coffee through the winter months as the pigeons came and went. in the spring he was no longer there, yet a wallet lay on the bench he used to sit on. the contents was two single dollar bills, an old credit card, and a faded drivers license. i flipped a snap from a small compartment that revealed some old black and white photos. they were wedding pictures of him and my mom before i was born. he waved at me the following October and i sat next to him listening to his story. it didn't make sense to me but i had to accept it as a fact of life. he took my hand as i led him out of the park. mom answered the door when i let them both say what each had to speak. it was now december as the xmas tree was lit with various presents that were never there before. mom and dad got back together and i was happy to see him, my father who i had never known. the three of us sat in the park every weekend feeding the pigeons and sipping on hot coffee, especially during the fall season when the leaves would change colors...

smooch + hug...

smooch + hug was often typed in the instant message screen. it also appeared in the mail that was sent to each over the course of about a year. sometimes we feel and know about each other before actually meeting in person. its like a plug that goes into an outlet with an instant connection. their time came in the middle of november when she would meet him. there was a smooch + hug in the middle of the street as horns honked them both to the reality of where they stood. holding hands on the short walk to his apartment was a testament to their already found connection. a small turkey they shared on thanksgiving and exchanged gifts on xmas eve. smooch + hug was now real as she moved in with him. her engagement ring sparkled behind the glass of wine that she held when they both toasted each other a happy new year. the church was filled with guests from both sides that were invited. after the priest blessed their wedding vows, they did something that was done so many times before. for them it was always the first time, a smooch + hug....

the company xmas party...

for a better word of being fired, let us say that michael was laid off or caught up in a budget cut from his company. it came at an unfortunate time, a week before christmas when most people are counting on their paycheck to survive and enjoy the holidays. he looked back on those ten years with fond memories of service and personal interactions with those employees who became very close friends. the company xmas party was always the same day and at the same place. december twenty first at a popular large restaurant with a look in front window. maybe it was a habit, maybe it was something more. michael stood outside and peered through the front look in window. there were new faces but also some old ones he recognized. susan looked out from within and remembered how he surprised her with a baby kitten for her daughters tenth birthday. fred reflected back when his coworker michael lent him money for a new car that was needed. janet stared out the window and thought back to when he saved her dog by driving fluffy to the vet hospital when he was hit by car while she wasn't home and he was. michael walked in but was stopped by a security guard who asked for an employee id. he turned around and walked back outside into the cold. a few people waved their arms from inside the front see through window. he looked down at his jacket to see his name tag attached and proceeded to return to the xmas company party. some old and new friends greeted him with tears in their eyes. nobody was sure whether it was the past or present or future, but it didn't really matter you see. among the guests without ids were some angels who need no clearance to be where they have to go. case in point where those who give shall receive...

the snow fell in 1972...

she was lucky to get to the liquor store just before it closed. he turned back on the lights and let his last customer in for one more sale. the year was 1970 and the month was december, just about nine PM. she browsed the shelves and decided on a popular brand of vodka for new years eve. he recommended a bloody Mary mix to go with it. "hey lady, this one's on me...happy new year", he said with a friendly smile. "thank you so much, you are very kind for that gesture", she replied. she paused at the front door and turned around with a wondering look in her eyes. maybe he read her mind as he then said, "you got any plans"? he closed up the store and the two of them walked out hand in hand like they knew each other before. it was december thirty first in her apartment where they sat an talked and laughed. the snow fell outside as they toasted in the new year. she went to bed in her room as he slept on the couch in her living room. in 1971 they awoke about the same time as he surprised his lady with a home made breakfast from her kitchen. she held his hand afterwards and thanked him for his respect of her. "i have somewhere to take you to before i go back home", he said. they walked about two blocks and he then covered her eyes and said, "its a surprise, don't look until we get into the store. she opened her eyes in a jewelry shop and he handed her a ring. that was where they had their second kiss and now it would be permanent. the snow fell in 1972 just outside a church a few blocks from where they both had lived....

a last dance shared

it was a last dance shared at a public school graduation. a kiss on each others cheek was a temporary goodbye. their eyes met in high school and remembered as the same dance continued. in a college the bond was established with now a kiss on the lips as adults often do. sometimes our first love becomes our last love also. there was an oldie song played at the wedding as the bride kissed the groom. i just happened to be a teacher as they grew up in all three phases of their education. my name is michael, just a guardian angel who dances in the lives of those who need to hear the music...

the night before...

you thought about him a few hours after reading his mail. it made you think and wonder and feel what was in his heart. there was a smile left on your pillow when you dozed off to sleep. his profile picture stuck in your mind and you wondered what he would be like in person. it was the usual distance and circumstances that kept us from meeting, but in a dream it was real as it comes. 1-800 - flowers delivered some roses at a time when you weren't home. a neighbor accepted them and gave them to you upon your return. he stood outside your door and watched from across the street. he stepped out of the car and walked towards you with a big smile on his face as you recognized a profile picture and a dream you had the night before...

when a campfire burned...

there was hotel he used to go as a little boy growing up. it was owned by his uncle and in the summer months they would spend many vacations together. mom and dad had long since passed away and the now 50 year old reflected on some of those memories. there was a new highway that led there as the old back roads were a thing of the past. the hotel kept its same name but obviously now under a different owner. it was in the off season when the place was closed and he parked his car in a lot without the usual attendant. snow covered the grass that blanketed a field which led to a site that he needed to go to. some old logs were there surrounded by stones which used to be a campfire during the summer months. it was a memory of his early teens where he held hands with then his first love. she parked her car in a lot during the off season when there was no attendant. the now 48 year old reflected on some memories from her childhood. she saw some flames in the distance

from the snow covered grass and walked forward.
he turned around and saw his dream come true.
it became a june wedding took place the following
summer. it was at night when a campfire burned...
and july once again as two old memories met for
a second kiss.

on roller skates...

the waitress was on roller skates and approached
the car at a drive in movie with their order. he
rolled down the window as the tray was placed
down. burgers and fries with 2 large cokes were
slowly consumed in the front seat through the first
half of the movie. the rest of the movie was missed
as the two of them slid into the backseats of his
car. young teens made out and kissed while the
volume on the microphone was turned down. this
was a memory of 1962 that never left my mind. a
shopping mall now stood in place where the drive
in movie used to be. however, the parking lot was
still there. I put an oldie station on the radio and
sat in the same spot as wishful thinking took over
my mind. the waitress was on roller skates and
approached my car with an order that was not yet
placed. "remember me"? she asked. the shopping
mall was suddenly gone and a big screen with a
familiar movie played again. my girl asked if we
could go back into the rear seat and make out.
some burgers and fries and 2 large cokes were left
on the front seat as we met again. time and love
needed to be shared when our memories needed

it the most. at our wedding the waitress was on roller skates...

goodnight sara jean...

sara jean was a collector of dolls. the old and the new ranging from raggedy ann and betsy wetsy to gi joe and whoever else you could think of. they all slept with her as some sat on the window sill of her bedroom. i tucked her in and carefully placed each doll where it was supposed to be. "goodnight sara jean", i said and kissed her on the forehead while she fell asleep. my 21 year old daughter was rushed to the hospital with a bad case of pneumonia. i brought her favorite dolls to the room she stayed in and placed them around her. she held one them in her hands before the nurse told me it was time to leave. i kissed her goodbye until the next visit was allowed. goodnight Sara jean. "daddy, i feel like i have to leave now", she said at my next visit. her eyes stared up at the ceiling and then went blank. i closed her lids and shed many tears that night as the nurse put her hand on my shoulder and led me away. i could see when i turned around that she was holding hands with something that looked like an angel to me. they both walked towards the window as two figures waved and smiled goodbye. the dolls still remain in her bedroom as i tuck her in and whisper "goodnight sara jean"....

between here and there...

after a year of chatting online and exchanging emails and phone calls, it was finally time to meet. i guess it was still a blind date since in person was never established. the halfway point that was decided happened during the xmas tree lighting ceremony in midtown manhattan. they both described what they would wear the night before so it would be easy to recognize each other. "you want mustard on that hot dog"? he asked as he smiled and she said "yes, thank you". they hugged and kissed for real and it was just as they imagined it from online. she canceled the stay at a motel as he invited her to stay with him at his place. his xmas tree already had a present beneath it which was planned in advance. the engagement ring fit perfectly on her finger as somewhere in a dream it already happened. new years eve was special for it was only online that they both celebrated it a year before. she saved a single rose on her computer from him but now it was real when he handed it to her in person. love finds a way to connect the dots between here and there...

randy...

randy was the name of a parakeet i gave to the black and green bird that mom and dad gave me on my tenth birthday. he was shy at first but eventually sat on my finger when i put it in the cage. fresh water along with bird seed was given ever day as i cleaned the cage when needed. he would chirp and sing along with the radio i played as if in tune with the music. randy eventually sat on my shoulder when i let him out of the cage a year later. he pecked gently on my ear which i knew was a kiss. on my twentieth birthday randy lay on the bottom of the cage with his feet up, a position of when a bird dies. mom and dad gave me permission to bury my friend in our back yard and i said a silent prayer over him. a few years later after i had moved out of my parents house, i set up my new apartment. the radio turned on by itself and a song from a long time ago played once again. chirping and singing echoed through the kitchen and i felt two small feet land on my shoulder. he pecked gently on my ear which i knew was a kiss....

the end is only the beginning...

it was the last story of his last book in a last chapter which had no title. his publisher filled it in after he had passed away. they titled it " the end is only the beginning". it ran for about 4 pages, more than the usual 1 or 2 his stories preceding ran. the title of his fifth and final book was called "before i go". they were short stories about the lives of fictional characters who had dreams of what needed to be done before they left the physical world. those last 4 pages were a thank you to his many fans and how his stories touched their lives in a special way. whether it be fate or coincidence, his book ended up in the hands of oprah winfrey. it was her favorite and she made a tv special about it as she interviewed his son. it was an emotional one hour show with phone calls lighting up the switchboard. his last book became a best seller as the first one "incredible short stories" and the second "where angels tread" soon followed. the author still writes in heaven now as a new fan club gathered around him. michael still signs autographs where the end is only the beginning...

took me home...

betty was born on xmas eve so it was a double celebration for years to come. a birthday cake plus presents under the tree. on her tenth birthday her life was cut short by a hit and run driver just outside her school. i stopped celebrating the holidays for it had no meaning anymore to me. her mother, my wife then passed on one week later. the snow fell outside my window one xmas eve as a tree suddenly appeared in the living room. under it was two gifts. a birthday cake with ten candles and my wife holding it before me. i decorated the tree for years to come and celebrated a time where we were all together once again. the snow fell outside my window as an angel took me home....

coney island revisted...

it was a place where time stood still. the beach, the boardwalk, the rides, and the smell of nathan's famous hot dogs and fries. a summer get away for adults and children alike. the place in question is coney island where smiles and laughter and all around fun takes us there. mom and dad took me there during the 50's and 60's and became embedded in my mind quite some years later. now it was 1995 and i felt the urge to go back there. my 56 year old body was still in the mind of a 14 year child when i got there. pink cotton candy swirled around a stick as it did before. i squeezed the plastic bottle of ketchup on my burger as also with my fries. of all the rides there, the merry go round was my favorite since it was slow as the painted horses went up and down to the piped in music. her 53 year old body remembered a place where mom and dad used to take her to during the 50's and 60's. her 11 year old mind brought her back there. the ride was full as one lady begged the attendant to let her on the ride. "ok he said, but you will have to double up and sit on the back of this horse with someone in front of you." she put her arms around my waist and rested her head on my shoulder. a memory from way back when it happened before. a second chance on love was found once again when two older bodies with the same young mind reconnected. in 2,008 me and my wife went back there with our two daughters and two sons. somehow they were attracted to the merry go round....

it was sara...

she slept on her right on the top of my computer shelf. one wing covered her left shoulder as she dreamed with a small smile on her face. it was a porcelain angel that I took with me throughout the years living from apartment to apartment. she was one foot wide from head to toe and maybe four or five inches high in width. she was witness to many a one night stand that i thought would last on my part. loneliness had me name her sara and i would talk to her often before i went to bed. one night maybe it was seen by me, some red lipstick and black mascara around her eyes. a painful memory of live people who came and went in my life. her wing seemed to open in my imagination and a tear ran down her cheek. and so a grown man takes a porcelain figure and places it on a night stand in his bedroom. he kissed her goodnight in his minds eye and drifted into sleep. i needed a maid to clean the apartment while i was away a lot and traveling at the same time. my ad was answered with a knock on my front door. her references were excellent and i hired her on the spot. she came twice a month and did a great job. my porcelain angel was

 missing one night from my bedroom night stand. the cleaning lady stood before me with red lipstick and black mascara around her eyes. "remember me"? she said as a tear ran down her cheek. i cried *and hugged and kissed her as a wing opened up and wrapped around me. it was sara...*

the old fashioned way...

don't you just love those forwards of jokes from 5,000 members? your buddy forgot how to send one on one mail for just you and him or her. so we become just a list of who to send mail to. I left the computer and wrote a letter with a pen and paper. then I sealed the envelope with a kiss and put an old fashioned postage stamp on it. the five days were worth it as I got a reply. we met in person for the first time as I handed her a single red rose. maybe a pen and a paper from one on one made a difference. we sent out invitations for our wedding the old fashioned way...

and we named her tweedy...

a baby bird fell out of its nest while i looked out my bedroom window one story above. i raced downstairs and opened the back door which led to the garden and trees of my parents home. my ten year old mind didn't know how to treat the bird, but my heart and soul wanted to save it. one leg was bent and one small wing was crooked. i gently picked her up and walked slowly back into the house calling out for mom and dad. that Saturday morning my parents drove us to the nearest animal hospital. "please save tweedy", i said to the first doctor who took her away from me. a week later she was fully recovered and i even offered my weekly allowance money to my parents to help pay for the bill. she chirped and flipped her little wings as little brown eyes smiled at me as only a ten year old and a baby bird could understand. dad set up a ladder and I climbed the tree when I gently put her back in the nest. i watched from my bedroom window as the mother fed her baby once again. the following summer there was a peck on my window and i opened it to let a mother and a daughter in. i guess it was a thank you of some sort and they both stayed with me for the next ten years. a photographer at my wedding caught something on film some fifteen years later as i kissed my bride. two birds over each of our shoulders were seen. maybe this is a testament for which love never dies. my wife gave birth to a little girl and we named her tweedy....

a xmas candle...

a xmas candle burned down half way on the window sill as the smell of pine filled the living room. amanda unwrapped the gift to herself of a medal of honor that she kept from the last 15 years. she thought back to when a letter from the state department had her husband missing in action from the vietnam war. she blew out the candle and went to bed. a prisoner of war was stripped of his identity and memory back then until he finally awoke back in the states recovering from shock and amnesia. civilian shoes which one was *combat boots stepped softly through the snow to a home he used to live at. he wondered if she would remember him. the doorbell rang and amanda got out of bed in the middle of the night, in the middle of a dream. a xmas candle re-lit itself at half way on the window sill from which it sat. she opened the door and they just stared at each other without saying a word. then came a hug and kisses that were 15 years missing. she placed an old medal of honor around his neck where it belonged. and so an angel guided some time lost and found in a home where an xmas candle burned down half way...*

once again...

it was a slow dance maybe from a memory, maybe from just a dream. if i held you close for real or only in my imagination, then so be it. all i know is that we did it together. just before the club closed there was a voice that announced "last call". maybe our distance and time finally met when i held you once again.

someone comes to a table...

the waitress came to his table with her cowboy hat and brown leather boots. it was in a small bar in a small town somewhere in texas. she served him a few beers with a smile, but her eyes seemed to be a little sad. she put a quarter in the jukebox during her 20 minute break and sat at a table across from him. the stranger from new york felt an attraction and asked her to dance to the slow songs that she had played. they danced together without saying a word, just held each other tight like it was the right thing to do. he took off his tie and she placed her hat on top of his head and the sadness left her eyes. ten or so people who were there turned their heads and watched them dance with a smile on their faces. it was a point in time when neither knew the other, but yet had to be together. she packed a small suitcase and put it in the trunk of his car. it was time to start a new life. on the way home he parked his car just in front of a jewelry store. he held her hand as they walked in and then pointed to a ring under the glass counter. one year later she kicked off her brown leather boots and he took off his wedding tie. she put her cowboy hat on top of his head and smiled with a loving tear in her eye. there was no live band but a surprise instead just behind the dance floor. he walked her to it as a familiar jukebox sat there that he had delivered to their special occasion. his bride put a quarter in it and they danced slow forever where sometimes someone comes to a table...

arizona doll...

there was a long stretch of highway while driving through arizona before i came to a gas station. "fill her up and please check the oil" i said to the attendant. he cleaned my front windshield first and then did the other chores. about fifty feet away was a small souvenir shop and i told the man i'll be back in about ten minutes or so. there was an american indian doll that stood about a foot high dressed in her original outfit which caught my attention. the details were so lifelike that I felt compelled to buy this item. the man that sold it to me appeared to be in his 70's and was also of indian heritage. "this doll was hand crafted in the likeness of my granddaughter at the age of seventeen, three years later she left me and disappeared." i said that i was very sorry to hear that and would take very special care of this fantastic piece of work. i stopped off at a bar about a hundred miles away on my journey. a 20 year stripper danced around a pole as her face looked so familiar. she took a short break and sat at a table next to mine. i went back outside and retrieved the doll from the front seat of my car. my hand placed it on the table where she sat and i said to her, "does this look familiar to you"? she shook her head no, but in her heart and her eyes, she knew it was her. "your grandfather misses you and wants to see again", i said to her. she put her hands around my neck and cried. we drove back about a hundred miles and got out at a gas station with a place about fifty feet away that needed to be seen again. she ran to him and apologized over and over as he hugged his granddaughter once again. the old man pointed out to me a necklace where in his tradition was an item of marriage. he gave it to me at no charge as little fawn, his granddaughter looked at me with expectant eyes. the gas station attendant cleaned my front windshield, changed the oil, and filled up the gas tank. my wife and i drove away as grandpa hand made two new dolls.... and so the beholder...

i am never lonely for I have myself. i seek not comfort from without, but from within. there is always a welcome mat and two pillows just in case, yet that is just a possibility. contentment is in the eyes of the beholder. and so the beholder wonders and thinks about what might be...

when a cat reads in heaven...

serena was my cat from july of 2,000 to sept 2,008. her life span should have been longer, but an illness took her away before her time. it was in july when i read to her a few stories each night from my first published book. she purred and seemed to understand what i spoke as my serena licked my face and fell asleep. one of those stories started on page 207 and ended on page 209 which was the last entry. it was about her and how we shared such love between a human and a pet. one year after her passing i heard the flipping of pages from a book that sat on my night table in the bedroom. it lay open to page 207 where it all began.

i heard a soft purr next to my pillow and felt a lick on my face...

the invitation...

after a few months he decided it was time to send out the invitation. it was carefully written in the mail where the love for her expressed a need to be together. her existence was content where she lived but not necessarily happy. she cried and welcomed it as a new beginning in a new place. two weeks into the month of January of 2,009 she settled in an apartment about 15 minutes away from where he lived. her housewarming gift was a bottle of her favorite wine as they clicked and cheered and kissed for the first time. she visited him also during the next few months as the dating had officially begun. one morning they both woke up next to each other on two pillows which had been a dream a long time ago. it was the month of April of the following year when they sent out the invitation. some of the guests drove, some took a bus or a train. a few flew in from another city. her thoughts were of a ring under a pillow the year before and how this all came to be. love finds a way in time and distance where what is supposed to happen will. maybe an angel guided his hand when he wrote the invitation...

a frog and a butterfly...

a frog sat on a lily pad with his big eyes and green body as he croaked his song. the butterfly looked down at him and thought to herself, what an ugly creature. he looked up at her and thought, what a lovely butterfly. so we do the same as people before getting to know the other. i turned back time when the frog was just a tadpole and the butterfly was a caterpillar. now on common ground they both looked good to each other. I watched over two people who thought the same way until I turned back the clock once again. two innocent young people held hands in a playground where we learn to love for its worth. her wings were there all the time and his eyes were always deep blue. my name is Michael and i am an angel. love sometimes needs to go back to the past in order to see the present. therefore we can continue in the future...

ribbit...

they would talk on the phone after knowing each other for some months now being friends online. friday was their make believe date night as both had a glass of wine on her end and a beer on his end. a burp would come up with him saying ribbit. she laughed out loud and said "i love you my frog". there came a time when she was ready to move and their love for each other had her 15 minutes away from where he lived. she called him on the phone to set up their first visit together. she sipped on her wine and he held a beer in his hand as they chatted. before they hung up and made plans to meet he felt a burp coming up and said ribbit. they both laughed again as she said "i love you my frog". online mail and chats became a reality as they dated often on weekends and sometimes during the week. the inevitable happened as a date was set the following summer for their marriage to be. it was a small wedding with an equal amount of guests from both sides. the priest asked the question of her "do you take this man to be your husband through sickness and in health, to love and cherish till death do you part"? " i do" she replied. "do you take this woman to be your wife through sickness and in health, to love and cherish till death do you part"? the crowd erupted into unexpected laughter as he replied with an unexpected burp which came out as ribbit. "i now pronounce you man and wife", the priest said with a smile and a laugh in his voice. the couple had their first slow dance together as the guests joined the floor. she whispered in his ear, "i love you my frog" as she unexpectedly burped ribbit....

the second autograph...

at the first book signing event, mom wheeled her 10 year old daughter to the front of the line. "she never liked to read before but since she picked up your book, she couldn't put down." i signed it with a personal note as her arms outstretched from the wheelchair and gave me hug around my neck. she was my most inspirational fan and it touched me deeply. mom waved back at me as held my first book "incredible short stories" in her hand. that little girl had me write a second book which was to be titled "where angels tread". two years later a message was left on my answering machine. "my daughter who is now 12 years old is very sick now and in the hospital. you signed her first book when i came to the front of the line with her in a wheelchair. remember us"? she left her phone number and i called her immediately. my trip to the hospital was as swift as i could get there. mom sat beside the bed and cried as i held her daughters hand. the little girl opened the book to a story about where we go when our time is up. my hand was steady although my heart was shaken when i signed the second autograph. she closed the book and whispered "thank you my angel". her arms hugged my neck and i told her to go towards the light. me and mom God were present when this sweet little soul had left us. my time came some years later and she was there to greet me. the little girl held out her second published book from heaven as i asked for her autograph....

let's hold hands...

i would like to replace the word "mourn" with the word "celebrate". tears of sorrow replaced with tears of joy. the death of a loved one is a new life for them where the physical body is no longer needed, yet the spirit and energy continue on. their presence is felt in a different way now, sometimes in a dream, sometimes a scent or a song on the radio. unexplained pennies left around the house where they shouldn't be. a butterfly or bird landing on your shoulder. heaven is not one million miles away but only 3 feet above our heads. lets hold hands....

whispering seashell...

it was the summer of 1965, the year we graduated high school. my ring sat on her finger as a token of our love from our senior year. we dated since our freshman year and young sweethearts established a four year relationship. in the middle of august we sat on a blanket at our favorite beach as she picked up a seashell and held it to her ear. the sound of waves were heard and she handed it to me as i listened also. next to me was another seashell and i picked it up as she did the same with hers. we both held them to our ears as if they were telephones. we both whispered "i love you forever" and it became part of the sound included with the waves. my magic marker drew our initials on both shells and i threw them back into the ocean. those were my memories of the love i had lost when she drowned that day. in 1985 i sat on a blanket at a beach we used to go to. the ring was kept by me which was the only possession that we once shared. a seashell washed ashore and sat silently in front of the blanket i sat on. the sound of waves were heard when i held it to my ear. there was nobody left on the beach that night when i walked towards the oncoming waves. "i love you forever" was the last thing i heard. they found me the following day washed up on the sand with shell in my hand. officer John Watson turned over and noticed some initials that remained af 20 years. a whispering seashell....

e
a
it
ter